DOUBLE CROSS TRAIL

E. E. HALLERAN

CHIVERS
THORNDIKE

This Large Print book is published by BBC Audiobooks Ltd, Bath, England and by Thorndike Press®, Waterville, Maine, USA.

Published in 2005 in the U.K. by arrangement with Golden West Literary Agency.

Published in 2005 in the U.S. by arrangement with Golden West Literary Agency.

U.K. Hardcover ISBN 1–4056–3453–7 (Chivers Large Print)
U.K. Softcover ISBN 1–4056–3454–5 (Camden Large Print)
U.S. Softcover ISBN 0–7862–7892–7 (British Favorites)

The text of this Large Print edition is unabridged.
Other aspects of the book may vary from the original edition.

Set in 16 pt. New Times Roman.

Printed in Great Britain on acid-free paper.

British Library Cataloguing in Publication Data available

Library of Congress Cataloging-in-Publication Data

Halleran, E. E. (Eugene E.), 1905–
Double cross trail / by E.E. Halleran.
p. cm.
"Thorndike Press large print British favorites."—T.p. verso.
ISBN 0–7862–7892–7 (lg. print : sc : alk. paper)
PS3515.A3818D68 2005
813'.54—dc22 2005013457

1

The westbound train was already two hours late when it shuddered to a halt in Abilene. Blue uniforms were in the cab of the fussing little locomotive while one of the passenger cars showed a solid line of blue arms and shoulders at its windows. Four civilian passengers descended from the rear coach to the patch of level ground which served as a station platform, a big man in a black frock coat and a flat-crowned black hat climbing the steps to replace them. Behind him a stout gentleman in a wrinkled sack coat, baggy pants and a fine glow of alcohol struggled to get aboard. A pair of solemn-faced cowboys went through elaborate motions of helping him with his baggage, contriving to annoy him and amuse the onlookers at the same time. Over it all a haze of dusty heat hovered and the trainman on the platform mopped his face wearily with a red bandana as he watched the loading crew throwing wood on the tender of the locomotive.

Farther along the platform another man was watching the fat man's troubles, chuckling a little to himself as he strode toward the express car. He was a wiry looking young fellow of slightly better than medium height, his lean, brown face showing lines which seemed oddly out of place on his otherwise youthful countenance. Even now, with the quirk of amusement around his mouth, he seemed older than his twenty-odd years. Those little crow's-feet at the corners of his eyes might simply be the result of much squinting into prairie sunlight, but the other lines indicated something more significant. There had been hardship and trouble in the young man's past, trouble which had left a mark that now showed through his smile. He wore clothing of Eastern cut, obviously new and not too well fitted, but the luggage he carried to the door of the express car consisted of a saddle, a slicker roll and one of those strapped containers which the cowboy referred to as his war bag.

He exchanged a quick pleasantry with the express messenger as he shoved the outfit into the baggage car, then strode back along the platform, paying no attention to the blue elbows in the coach windows just above his head. Uniforms had once held a prominent place in his life but that was a part of the past which he preferred to forget. Ignoring them now was a part of his forgetting.

He climbed to the front platform of the rear coach just as a whoop from the other end indicated that the playful cowpunchers had finally boosted their inebriated victim to the top of the car steps. The coach was full, frontiersmen, cattle buyers, emigrants and other assorted citizens filling almost every seat with their persons and baggage. The young man stepped around the gun rack which the railroad company had installed at the end of the car, his quick glance noting that they had provided the cheapest protection possible. The weapons were breech loaders, all right, but they were needle guns of French manufacture. Neither safe nor dependable.

His gray eyes narrowed a little as he looked for a seat. There seemed to be three vacant places near the far end of the car but as he started toward them the fat man lurched clumsily into one. The other half of that particular seat was occupied by a brown-haired girl in her early twenties and he caught the flash of disgust in her eyes as the fat man fell against her. An elderly man across the aisle said something in a low voice and the inebriate turned to curse him. The girl pulled her cape about her and shrank against the window. There was no smile left on the young man's oddly lined face as he moved toward the scene of the disturbance.

Somebody laughed nervously and the fat man seemed to think he had an appreciative audience. He grinned foolishly, belched with great gusto and let his weight fall against the girl, one of his fat red hands reaching out to cover hers. The girl's brown eyes closed momentarily but then she pulled herself together and smiled determinedly up at the approaching stranger. 'I'm sorry, Joe,' she said clearly, her eyes eloquent. 'I tried to save the seat for you but this gentleman seems to think he should have it.'

The young fellow did not even blink at this totally unexpected greeting. It fitted in too well with his own intentions. 'His mistake,' he said calmly. 'Mister, you wouldn't mind moving over to another seat, would you? I sorta had a claim staked here.'

The mildness of the request seemed to puzzle the fat man. He frowned and glanced about him. Other people were watching, waiting to see whether their new and noisy fellow traveler would maintain his belligerence. The fat man seemed to sense the expectancy—and be annoyed by it. 'Got a right to take any damn seat I want,' he said thickly. 'My seat. G'way.'

The young fellow did not even glance at the girl. He was concentrating on the drunk, his tone almost benevolent as he murmured, 'You're sure you want it that way, Mister?'

'G'way, I tell ya,' the fat man repeated more loudly, as though confident that he could outface this young meddler. 'Ain't no r'served seats on this train. G'way.'

A lean hand fastened itself promptly in the bulging shirt front and the fat man came out of the seat so suddenly that his hat flew off. Instantly he was whirled around to be trundled up the aisle and into another vacant place. There was just time for him to emit one gasping curse and then he was firmly planted beside the broad-shouldered man who had boarded the car just ahead of him.

'Sorry to inflict this fellow on you,' the young fellow said quietly to the big man. 'If he crowds you too much just punch him in the belly. I reckon you're big enough to take care of yourself.'

Strangely enough, the big man seemed pleased. He nodded smilingly, one heavy hand closing on the fat man's arm. 'We'll get along fine,' he said, his voice noteworthy for the way he seemed to clip off every syllable so precisely.

'Good enough,' the younger man said. He took a couple of quick strides, picked up the fat man's hat and returned just as that irate gentleman was struggling to arise. The hat went back into place with sufficient force to settle the fat man for a second time. Then the young fellow spoke again, a hint of iron in the even tones now. 'Sit still,' he ordered. 'If I have to come back again I might get rough.'

The big man winked gravely and took a tighter grip on his new seat-mate.

Nobody laughed. The young fellow went quietly back to the girl, his tones mild again as he smiled down at her. 'That's what you get for being beautiful,' he said aloud, as he sat down. 'Even fat drunks want to sit with you.'

She blushed prettily, all too well aware that every eye was upon them. Her voice was steady, however, as she played the act through, 'I'm glad you appreciate me,' she laughed. 'I just wish you wouldn't be so late all the time and get me into these messes.'

'Sorry,' he told her. 'I'll never do it again.'

The train jolted into motion then and they were able to talk without being overheard. Some of her poise seemed to desert her as she murmured, 'I don't know how to thank you for that—and I'm sorry to have caused you the trouble. You took your cue beautifully.'

'No trouble at all,' he assured her. 'All my life I've dreamed of something like this happening to me but this is the first time I ever came close to it. Are you going very far?'

She studied him a moment before replying, apparently trying to decide whether he was going to be a new problem. Finally she laughed, half in annoyance. 'You work almost as fast as our fat friend. Don't let this encourage you, but I'm going as far as the train does, I expect.'

'Sheridan? That's the end of the line, isn't it?'

'Yes—but since these Indians started raiding along the rail line they haven't been running any trains at night. They stay over at whatever station they happen to be approaching when darkness catches them. Unless we make up a lot of time I don't see how we can do any better than to reach Hays City.'

‘And you live there?’

‘That’s right. So you see I’m not worried about the train being late unless it fails to reach Hays.’

‘Good,’ he said calmly. ‘Hays City happens to be my destination too. My luck is certainly in today. By the way, my name is Malloy—Sid Malloy. Maybe it’s not as nice a name as Joe but I have to put up with it.’

‘I’m sorry,’ she said quickly. ‘That was the first name that popped into my mind when I decided to be so bold.’

‘I hope you didn’t have too big a reason for having it on your mind,’ he murmured.

Again she studied him, seriousness giving her narrow face a severity which had not been apparent when she smiled. Malloy decided that she was not really beautiful. Her chin was too pointed and her face was too thin as it tapered from the broad forehead. Then she smiled, the smile breaking up all the angularity, and he changed his mind. Maybe she did not have classical beauty but there was a liveliness about her features which he liked. It was the same with her hair and eyes. Both were brown but deceptively so. Just about the time he had them classified there would come a sparkle which forced him to alter the appraisal. The eyes had a glint which reminded him of flecks of gold but the high lights in her hair were pure copper. Almost lost in the mental inventory he caught himself up with a start as he realized that she was reciprocating his introduction of himself.

'My name is Helen Temple,' she told him almost primly. 'My folks run an eating house in Hays City. I've been to Kansas City on a buying trip.'

'You picked a good time to go,' he said. 'Otherwise I'd have had to wait several hours before meeting you. Of course I would have met you in Hays anyway but this makes it much more convenient, don't you think?'

She tried to put a shade of annoyance in her short laugh. 'Do you always give the girls a quick line of talk like this? When I spoke for your help I thought you were a serious-minded man who would remain that way.'

'And you were perfectly right. Maybe it doesn't sound like it but I'm certainly being serious right now.'

She shook her head slowly with a gesture of resignation.

'Well, at least you don't take up as much room as that other man.'

His long fingers stretched out straight before him as he flattened his hands on the knees of his trousers. 'I suppose I deserved that cut,' he observed without rancor. 'Maybe I'm a bit too exuberant today. My luck has been turning for the better and I hardly know how to act; it's been bad for so long. Forgive me and tell me about Hays City. Whom should I look up to get a line on the nearby settlers?

I'm hunting an old friend of mine named Hod McIntyre.'

'That's better,' she said. 'I think we can continue to be friendly—but I don't know any McIntyre.'

He smiled a little at her tone. This girl certainly knew her own mind. She had kept her wits about her when the fat man tried to force his company upon her; now she was showing her self-possession in still another way. 'You're a pretty cool hand,' he told her. 'I'll bet if we have an Indian raid this afternoon you'll be the first to rush for one of those railroad rifles.'

She smiled as she shook her head. 'I would do nothing of the sort,' she contradicted. 'In case you didn't notice, the rifles are chained to the rack so that passengers can't use them to shoot buffalo out of the car windows. I would wait until the conductor unlocked them.'

He laughed aloud. 'Correction accepted. But you prove my point for me. About keeping a cool head, I mean.'

She smiled and said nothing so he asked a question. 'Have there been any raids around your part of the state this fall?'

'No. The town is pretty close to Fort Hays and when the Indians come our way they're very, very peaceful fellows.' Her lips tightened as she added, 'It was one of those lovely peaceful groups that went north to commit those massacres on the Saline and Solomon last month.'

He nodded gravely. 'That was the raid that brought forth General Sheridan's declaration of war on the Cheyennes, wasn't it? Sort of a silly gesture, it seemed to me.'

She frowned. 'Why so?'

'Only that I can't see any reason for getting formal over an Indian fight. The Indians have always raided when they felt like it and suffered their punishment when they could be caught. I don't expect they'll ever change and I can't see the point in the army going formal just when the worst of the raiding is about over for the season.'

'But is it over?'

'Of course. This warm weather is bound to break before many days and when it does every Indian on the prairie will sneak into a peaceful village and make long speeches about how he loves the white brother. Indians don't have the organization to fight in winter.'

'You talk like an old Indian fighter,' she told him half humorously.

'Only Comanches,' he replied. 'I'm just saying what is common knowledge. I have to talk about something to keep you from ignoring me.'

This time she laughed merrily and they talked of many subjects without either of them touching on personal affairs. Suddenly Malloy realized that the warm October afternoon had slipped almost entirely away. There had been no alarms and the rack of needle guns at the front end of the car had not been disturbed. In some way the raiding Cheyennes seemed to know that the train today was crammed with armed men.

Dusk was beginning to settle across the rolling prairie when Helen Temple nodded toward a sod house which crouched furtively under a swell of the land. 'There's Tod Digby's place,' she observed. 'That means we're getting close to Hays City.'

'Too soon,' Malloy observed. Then, before she could reprove him, he added, 'And not a shot fired all afternoon. I understood that there was some kind of a fracas along the tracks every time the train came along.'

'There has been enough trouble,' she told him grimly. 'Of late, however, the Indians seem to have given up hope of a successful attack on the railroad. They don't seem to understand how to go about it and the railroad guards have beaten them pretty badly a couple of times. It's the poor settlers who have been taking the brunt of the raids.'

'I'm not complaining,' Malloy assured her. 'I've had my fill of fighting and if I never see an Indian I'll be completely happy. For the rest of my life I'm planning to be a peaceful citizen with a hankering to watch fat steers wading around in grass up to their bellies.' There was a seriousness behind the words which belied the lightness of his tone.

Her laugh conveyed a similar impression. Like Malloy, she seemed to be remembering something which she preferred to gloss over with the light touch. 'You won't be staying in Kansas then,' she said. 'They fatten steers on this prairie grass but nobody seems to think much of the country for general cattle raising.'

'You guessed it,' he retorted. 'I figure to see this fellow McIntyre and then I'm headed west to mountain country. I like to look at something besides distance—and yowling heathens.'

A trainman came through then, warning the passengers that they would not proceed beyond Hays City until the following morning. All around them travelers began collecting their bundles while just ahead Malloy could see the big man in the black coat trying to arouse the sleeping fat man. For a moment it brought his mind back to a matter he had not taken the time to consider. When he had hauled the inebriate out of the seat his hand had touched a hard object which he saw was a silver badge. That fat fellow must be an officer of some sort. What could he be doing out here on the frontier—and in his present condition? For that matter, why had the big man been so happy to take care of him?

The girl interrupted his thoughts. 'You're coming to dinner with me, of course,' she said in a matter-of-fact tone. 'My folks would disown me if I didn't bring the man who saved me from a thoroughly disagreeable afternoon.' Her smile broke out again. 'Really, we have the best food in Hays City.'

He waited until the engineer had finished whistling for brakes. 'Any excuse would be good enough for me,' he retorted, catching her eye for the first time in many minutes. 'I was just wondering how I was going to make sure that you didn't get away from me.'

'Don't make me sorry I asked you,' she warned.

They made their way to the dirt platform as the train clanked to a halt, working out through the crowd as quickly as possible. 'I have to get my duffle from the express car,' he explained. 'Will you wait or shall I follow along later?'

'I'll go ahead.' She motioned toward a square, frame building which seemed to face away from the railroad. 'That's the Prairie Hotel,' she said. 'If you're looking for a room it's no worse than the others and it's better than some.'

She broke off, a little embarrassed. 'You do want a room, I suppose?'

His smile was completely good-natured. Once more he found himself reading the thought in those brown eyes. She was afraid that he was not ready to meet the cost of hotel accommodations. 'Thanks for the advice,' he told her. 'And don't worry about me. I'm a bloomin' duke in disguise. The poke is plumb full.'

She nodded, still not sure of herself. 'Very well then. Our place is right across the lane from the hotel on the south side. I'll be waiting for you.'

'I'll be along pronto,' he promised. 'Just give me time to cart my traps over to the hotel and wash some of the cinders off of my neck.'

She smiled and started out into the dusty street which led toward the buildings of the town's main street. He watched her for a moment, then strode toward the baggage car, skirting the file of troopers who were forming ranks on the station platform. It was not until he was almost at the door of the express car that he looked back over his shoulder. What he saw took the glint out of his eyes and the last trace of smile from his lips.

Helen Temple was being greeted by a tall, slender man in boots and flannel shirt. The greeting left little to the imagination. The man had taken her into his arms and was kissing her in a manner which left little doubt as to their relationship. The bright dreams of the afternoon were over.

2

A warm, dusty darkness had fallen across Hays City when Sid Malloy came out of the side door of the Prairie Hotel. He had taken plenty of time with the brief business of washing away the train dirt and changing into a clean shirt. Had he followed his real inclinations he would have delayed even longer. Much as he hated to admit it, he had let himself go overboard for a pretty face—only to see that face being kissed by a young man who didn't go about the matter like a relative. Now he had to go over and play the cheerful idiot, probably to watch Helen Temple holding hands with the tall young fellow who had greeted her so warmly. It was not a happy way to wind up an afternoon which had started with so much bright promise.

He lingered for a brief moment at the side door of the bar, then shook his head half angrily and moved out into the darkness of the alley. Lights gleamed from windows on both sides of the main street, but for some reason Malloy could sense a false note in the commonplace evening scene. The town was too quiet. There ought to be plenty of noise in a wide-open frontier community at this time of night. Instead there was an almost oppressive silence. It wasn't natural.

He stood at the corner for a moment before moving down the sidewalk past the front entrance of the hotel. There were plenty of people in sight, little knots of dark figures huddled at store fronts and on corners, all of them deep in conversations which seemed to be entirely whispers. In the yellow lamplight he could also see a plentiful scattering of blue uniforms among the more sombre shades of frontier garb and for a moment he assumed that the newly arrived troops had been given a bit of time to see the town before they marched out to the fort. Then he realized that most of the troopers in sight wore the insignia of the provost guard. Something must be wrong in town.

At almost the same moment his glance caught the sign hung from the wooden awning of a hardware store across the street. It proclaimed the place to be recruiting headquarters for the Nineteenth Kansas Volunteers (Cavalry). The final word had evidently been an afterthought of the sign painter; it crowded the edge of the canvas banner and was in cruder characters than the balance of the sign. More striking than the sign itself, however, was the scene in the lighted shop behind it. A table in there did duty as a desk and the round-bodied man who sat behind it wore a uniform which Malloy could not identify. The pair of troopers who lounged near him, however, were clad in the familiar blue of the regulars.

United States Cavalry. That was an odd one. Regulars on duty at a recruiting post for state militia. There seemed to be only one answer to that picture, Malloy decided. Border troubles had taken a turn for the worse. Certainly they seemed to be taking General Sheridan's proclamation seriously in Hays City.

He continued beyond the hotel and crossed the lane to where a lighted window bore the painted legend GEM RESTAURANT. It was not a very big place and just now there were only four persons in sight within. Two men in ordinary plains garb were seated together at a rear table; a third, wearing the uniform of a lieutenant of cavalry, stood at the cashier's table—and the fourth person was Helen Temple herself, acting as cashier.

Again Malloy caught the suggestion of tension in a situation which might have been so ordinary. There did not seem to be a thing wrong with the scene before him but he felt sure that the two men in the rear were watching the soldier with distrust and anger. The whole thing was just a fleeting impression, gained in the instant when he was reaching for the latch of the door.

A pleasant odor of food came to his nostrils as he went in but he noted it absently, intent on the quick action which flared before him. The stocky lieutenant was laughing loudly at something, reaching out with a swift hand to pinch Helen Temple's cheek. Something in the sound of the laugh rang a dim bell in Sid Malloy's memory but there was no time for him to think about it. Already the tall young fellow who had welcomed the girl so warmly near the station was lunging across the room. Malloy saw that he was a sallow-faced youth of about twenty-two, a lad whose thin features were regular enough to be called handsome. Now, however, the features were contorted with fierce anger as he grabbed the soldier's arm.

'No, Dave!' the girl cried sharply, some of her own anger fading before open anxiety for the boy.

The words had no effect. The lieutenant whirled swiftly, his footwork and the efficiency of his body motion proclaiming his ability as a boxer. He did not wait to see what the tall boy was going to do, but simply lashed out with a solid blow to the point of the lean jaw. There was not even a grunt, merely a crash as the young fellow hit the floor. It was all so calm and deadly that Malloy felt something of a chill go through him. Then he caught a glimpse of the lieutenant's hard, sneering face and an entirely different emotion seized him.

'Bad manners,' the lieutenant was saying to Helen Temple, an air of jauntiness quickly assumed. 'Your friend is too abrupt with his hands.'

She ignored him, already hurrying around the end of the counter toward the man on the floor. It was Malloy's voice which gave the soldier his answer, a soft, drawling voice which a certain drunken passenger might well have recalled. 'Still handy with your fists, I see, Loeffler,' he commented. No one would have guessed at any bitterness behind those casual words.

The stocky lieutenant knew, however. He whirled to face Malloy, his blunt features working with an emotion that was something more than mere surprise. A little vein in his broad forehead had swelled, pulsing noticeably as the color came to his face. Malloy saw the vein and remembered. It was a good sign. Walter Loeffler's anger was bordering on fear when that vein began to pulse.

The lieutenant swallowed hard before putting careful menace into his retort. 'Don't butt in, Malloy!' It was as though he warned against continuing a quarrel which had but recently ended.

'I never butt in,' Malloy told him, still in that same flat, emotionless tone. 'Not in other folks' affairs, that is. Of course there's some matters of my own I could take up any time now.'

The boy on the floor had regained consciousness quickly and was sitting up, Helen Temple supporting him with an arm about his shoulders. Malloy was aware that the fourth man in the room had come to his feet but he did not let anything divert him from that worried, bitter face so close to his own. It didn't pay to take your eyes off Walter Loeffler.

Oddly enough, he felt a peculiar amusement at himself as he stood there, amusement at the way he was acting in the unexpected emergency. Many times he had planned what he would say and do if he should ever meet Loeffler again. None of the things was pretty. But he wasn't doing any of those things he had dreamed about. He was just standing there—and somehow it seemed like the right thing to do. His very calmness was unnerving the stocky man more than any threat or action would have done. It was rather amusing to watch Loeffler's imagination working on him.

The lieutenant swallowed hard again, then blustered as though unable to contain himself any longer. 'Don't you try to threaten me, Malloy!' he barked. 'You're not running this town. There's law here, you know.'

It didn't seem like a particularly significant remark and Malloy smiled thinly, pleased at what he saw on his old enemy's face. 'You're afraid, Walter,' he said quite pleasantly. 'You're seeing a lot of things coming up to haunt you that you thought were left behind. I didn't die after all.' He took a single step forward, one of those long fingers pointing straight at Loeffler's broad nose. 'I lived to come back to face a dirty coward who . . .'

Loeffler's self-control gave way before that brief advance. He had been on the ragged edge of an explosion, disconcerted by the surprise of it all and baffled by Malloy's calmness. Now he fell back on the physical courage which was his. He sprang forward, brushing at the accusing finger with his left hand as he launched a crushing blow with his right, a blow powerful enough to have felled Malloy as abruptly as the similar punch had dropped the tall boy.

He was facing a different man now, however. Malloy rolled his head just enough to let the blow go over his shoulder, the motion seeming to be part of another movement which ended in a powerful uppercut. Loeffler was caught off balance from his own swing and the counterblow landed flush on the square chin, the impact loud in a room where the onlookers held their breaths. It straightened the lieutenant up abruptly and as he teetered on his heels for a split second Malloy drove home another hard punch to the chin. This time Loeffler did not even grunt. He went over backward with a resounding crash, to lie still beside the thin youth. The skirmish had been almost as brief as the earlier one.

Malloy blew thoughtfully on his knuckles as Helen Temple pulled the tall lad to his feet. Then he glanced down at the slack mouth of his antagonist, smiled wryly but without any mirth and turned to meet the worried brown eyes of the girl. ‘Sorry, Miss Temple,’ he said gently. ‘I didn’t mean to turn your restaurant into a battlefield.’

‘I’m glad you did,’ she retorted, catching her breath again. ‘You did just the right thing—but I don’t believe you should stay here. That fellow will cause plenty of trouble when he wakes up.’

Again Malloy’s smile concealed an emotion that was not mirth. ‘He has already been causing trouble,’ he replied. ‘I don’t think I’ll start worrying about him now.’

‘You better,’ the tall boy muttered, speaking as though his jaw still ached. ‘There’s martial law in town and the provost guard has been pretty rough with anybody interfering with a man in uniform. They’ll want to run you in for this.’

Malloy hesitated but the girl gave him no opportunity for reply. ‘Come along,’ she ordered briskly, evidently having made up her mind. ‘The pair of you can go out the back way until we get this business cleared up.’

The other man in the room came forward then and Malloy saw that he was a lanky fellow of about forty, a man who would have been quite tall if he had not been so stooped. From bow legs to round shoulders he seemed to droop in every part of his narrow body, but there was plenty of life in the faded blue eyes. ‘Go with the lady,’ he said, winking at Malloy. ‘I’ll stay here with the soljer and soothe his achin' head when he wakes up. Git now!'

Malloy grinned and started to follow Helen Temple and the tall youth toward a rear door. The stooped man's drawl cut in again, this time with more urgency. 'Better make tracks,' he advised. 'From here I got a right purty view of a feller talkin' to them troopers across the way. Judgin' by his motions in this direction he musta seen what happened in here.'

Under the circumstances it was a little ridiculous that Malloy's thoughts should be occupied with the coppery gleams in the brown hair just ahead of him. The lamplight did things for Helen Temple just as the afternoon sunshine had done.

A plump woman in a big apron met them at the kitchen door. 'What's wrong, Helen?' she asked worriedly, her attention divided between Malloy and the man on the floor.

'Nothing now,' the girl said briefly. 'A soldier started to get fresh and this gentleman hit him. We don't want any trouble with the patrols so the boys are going out the back way.'

'Do you really think it's necessary?' Malloy asked. 'I don't like the idea of running away—especially when I had a dinner engagement.' He caught the girl's embarrassed glance and added with a smile, 'And I'm hungry as a bear.'

Behind them the gaunt man snapped, 'Hurry it up!' and someone shouted from the street. Apparently the tension in town could be explained easily enough. Citizens and soldiers were not on very good terms with each other and at the present time the army was giving the orders.

The older woman stepped aside to let them pass and the girl spoke swiftly as she scooped up some biscuits and a few slices of ham. 'This is Dave Nixon,' she told Malloy. 'Go along with him. Dave, this is the man who helped me on the train this afternoon. You'd better hide in the stable until the fuss is over.' There was no particular excitement in her voice, only the hastiness of someone who recognizes the need for prompt action. Malloy saw that her lips had lost some of the tightness which he had seen back there in the dining room. She even managed to smile as she handed him the packet of food. He saw no reason to change his earlier appraisal of her; she was a girl worthy of a man's careful attention.

He followed Nixon through the back entrance even as a noise from in front indicated the arrival of the provost guard. In the darkness of the back yard the troubled voice of his companion came softly. 'Straight back this way. We'll hole up in the stable. If they start to search it we can dodge around and keep ahead of them. I reckon they won't look far, though.'

There was an odd note in the boy's voice which Malloy could not quite identify. Somehow the young fellow seemed to be sulking and Malloy wondered whether he was resentful of the unheroic part he had played. He had looked bad before his girl while another man was setting himself up as her champion. To Malloy the interpretation did not seem quite satisfactory. He had not fought with Loeffler because of anything that had happened this evening. Maybe he was getting credit for having defended Helen Temple's dignity, but he knew in his own heart that such was not the case.

A one-story building loomed blackly before them as they picked their way across a littered yard. The tall youth went directly to a small door at one side. Malloy halted instead of following him through the opening. 'Hold up a minute,' he said in a low voice. 'This is far enough for now. We'd better listen a minute and see what's happening back there.'

The boy grunted unintelligibly and the pair of them stood in the doorway, listening to the sound of angry voices from the restaurant. One of those voices was certainly that of Walter Loeffler. The burly lieutenant had regained consciousness and was shouting angry orders.

Then the shouts subsided and hurrying footsteps sounded in the night. The hunt was on. Malloy could trace the movement to the kitchen and presently Helen Temple's voice came in quiet defiance. 'Of course I helped them leave the place. They went out this door. Now get your men out of here and stop cluttering up the kitchen or I'll report you to the officer in charge.'

Nixon grunted again, anger and satisfaction blending in the sound. 'I can just see her giving them that haughty stare. She can sure do it to perfection when she wants to cut somebody down a peg.'

Malloy did not reply. He wondered how Nixon had acquired that particular bit of information but he did not think it diplomatic to inquire. Then he saw the back door of the kitchen thrown open to disclose a man with a lantern. The yellow rays gleamed on a yellower stripe down the man's trouser leg and Malloy slipped through the doorway into the stable, closing the door all but a tiny crack behind him. Troopers were making a search.

Another lantern appeared in the lane, a dark blur of figures following it into the back yard of the restaurant. Loeffer's voice issued sharp orders and the nasal drawl of the stooped man offered advice about hunting in the shadows behind the Prairie Hotel. Immediately the search party divided and there was an erratic pattern of lantern movement to indicate a hasty search in the various nooks and crannies at the rear of the adjacent buildings. Three dark figures plodded slowly toward the stable.

Malloy kept the door open just wide enough for him to watch developments. Apparently the three men who had come toward him were not keen on blundering around in the darkness. They halted within five yards, conversing disgustedly in low tones while the other searchers combed back yards for some distance in either direction.

Then the nasal voice sounded again, this time from a considerable distance to the south. 'Hey there, lootenint! Here's a feller says them two jiggers hustled off down this way. Want to talk to him?'

Loeffler bellowed a command to wait and Malloy almost laughed aloud. That scrawny old rascal was having himself a lot of fun distracting the attention of the military. A patter of running feet indicated that the diversion was succeeding, but Loeffler snapped a sharp command at the three men near the stable. 'May be a false alarm,' he said. 'You men stand guard here. One of you keep watch on the yards while the other two check up on the building. Keep alert!' Then he was gone in the darkness and Malloy could hear him searching profanely for the man who had reported the fugitives. Judging by the language he was using he could not even find the fellow who had relayed the report.

Slower footsteps came into the yard then and the nasal voice drawled good-humoredly, 'Sure do have big times in the army nowadays, sojers. It must take a full company to keep these here popinjay officers outa trouble. Good thing there ain't no more Injuns than there is. Between Injuns and second lootenints yo' never would git no time to play poker.'

One of the troopers laughed and another spoke cautiously, evidently in complete agreement with the sentiment expressed but careful about being overheard. 'Officers are the worst,' he grunted. 'You can shoot an Injun if he gets uppity.'

There was a subdued laugh and the nasal voice asked, 'Any luck with the hunt so far?'

A trooper spat noisily. 'No. And I hope the boys don't have any. That laddybuck what slugged the lieutenant ought to get a medal. Me, I'd buy him a drink if I could find him.'

'Noble sentiment,' the nasal voice approved. 'Sorry I ain't got time to chin with yo' no longer. Got a bronc to rub down. If yo' want to come in with me while I light a lantern and git to work it'll look like yo're searchin' the buildin'. Might as well make yoreselves look good.'

'That Andrews is a card,' the tall youth whispered in Malloy's ear. 'He'll keep 'em busy.'

3

They settled down on some grain sacks, listening as the conversation moved from the yard into the opposite end of the stable. The man who had been referred to as Andrews was keeping up a steady line of chatter and the three troopers seemed willing to let him do the talking. They had followed him to the stable door, evidently taking up positions where they could put on a quick show of activity should an officer appear.

'Git any new recroots lately?' Andrews inquired after talking about other unimportant topics for some minutes.

'A couple,' one of the troopers replied. 'Two burned out settlers decided that they owed the redskins somethin' and could get square better with the army. I dunno what good they'll be in a tight spot but they're plumb fired up and scrappy right now.'

'They'll do,' the stooped man replied with calm decision. 'I fought 'side o' some fellers like that last month and they sure handled their share o' the scrap.'

'Yeah? Where was all that?'

'Up on the Arickaree.'

One of the soldiers whistled. 'You with Forsyth?' His tone indicated a new respect.

'Yep. I ain't got fed up proper since. A man gits mighty puny livin' on over-ripe hoss meat fer so long.'

'That was a good fight,' the trooper approved. 'Still in the Scouts, are ye?'

'Hope.'

'Ye oughta be. We'll be needin' plenty o' scouts before this fuss is over.'

The sound which came from Andrews' lips

indicated disbelief. 'I reckon there won't be much more fightin' this year,' he drawled. 'It's too late in the season fer campaignin'.'

'Then why all this recruitin'?' the trooper demanded. 'It ain't like the army to haul in men unless they got a good use fer 'em. I got a hunch we'll do some ridin' in the snow this year.'

'It's a happy thought,' Andrews conceded politely. 'Luck to yo'.' There was a period of silence and then a rasping hum came to the listeners' ears. Malloy frowned perplexedly in the darkness, trying to identify the sound, but his companion nudged him gently, chuckling as though the sound had brought him out of his moodiness. 'Andrews is going to sing,' he whispered. 'It will be awful. It always is.'

It was. The nasal voice never quite managed to make a tune of it, mere volume failing to overcome the complete lack of pitch. Malloy's grin widened as he listened. He could not decide whether the singer was improvising his tune as well as his lyrics but certainly no part of it was familiar. Malloy decided that he was just as happy to have it so; familiarity with such a performance was not to be desired.

'There's a Texas gal a-waitin'
Where the Pecos flows so free,
Full of alkali and quicksand
And I know she waits fer me.
Waits fer me, waits fer me.

Purty soon I'll go a-ridin' back to Tex-as.'

'Are you sufferin'?' a trooper asked caustically, 'or is it just us?'

Andrews did not deign to dignify the question with an answer. He simply droned into what appeared to be a second stanza.

'Her hair's a purty yeller
And her eyes are kinda blue.
With dainty hands she blacked my eye
So I know she loves me true.
Loves me true, loves me true . . .

Two new sounds interrupted the concert. One was the tramp of feet at a little distance and the other was the noise of three troopers acting busy.

'Riley!' a voice hailed.

'Here, sarge.'

'See anything of him around here?'

'Not a thing. We went all through the stable and hunted both sides of it careful.'

'Come along then. It ain't likely he stayed around. The lieutenant is trying all the saloons down the street.'

The voices dropped as the men moved out toward the newcomer. 'Wonder why he's so all-fired anxious to ketch up with that jasper?' one of the troopers asked. 'It ain't the army's job to settle his private scores for him.'

'Shut up!' the sergeant snapped. Then, in a

lower tone, he added, 'The lieutenant's makin' a fool of himself, if ye ask me. I never seen a man so shakin' mad, though. It's lucky we didn't find that feller; there mighta been murder done.'

Quiet descended upon the stable yard, only the nasal humming from the stalls indicating that anyone remained in the vicinity. The young fellow poked Malloy in the ribs. 'Might as well go on in there with Andrews,' he said, his sulkiness again apparent in his voice. 'It looks like the big hunt is all over.'

Malloy followed without comment, wondering at the boy's attitude. Certainly the youth had looked a little foolish back there in the restaurant, but there was no reason for him to be so childish about his misfortune. No one was trying to make capital of his situation.

They went through a doorway into a room where the lantern's smoky rays disclosed a series of stalls and the usual odds and ends to be found in a stable. Instantly the nasal voice stopped its drone and the stooped man turned to present an amused grin. 'Looks like the army has went back to barracks.'

'Thanks to your genial efforts,' Malloy told him. 'I can see that you're a man of ideas. Maybe you can even tell me how come the provost rides herd on this town.'

'Easy enough,' Andrews chuckled. 'The town marshal, a gent name of Hickok—Will Bill, the boys call him—is takin' hisself a holiday in some sink hole of iniquity farther east. With Bill away the boys started to play—and they got rough. So the army steps in, claimin' they got to pertect us pore civilians from each other, seein' as how there's a shore enough war goin' on not so danged far away. Bill oughta be back any day now. Then the sojers kin go back to fightin' Injuns—if it don't snow too soon.'

'I heard your talk on that last point,' Malloy remarked. 'Has the raiding been very close to Hays?'

'Tol'able close, I hear. I ain't been around here long myself.'

'Long enough to know anything about a place called Wild Run Creek? I'm looking for a friend of mine who homesteaded a quarter section there. Gent by the name of Hod McIntyre.'

Andrews scratched a lean chin on which the stubble shone coppery in the lamplight. 'I can't say fer sure but it seems like I heard tell o' Wild Run Crick. Ain't it somewhere up along the Solomon?'

'I wouldn't be surprised. Almost due north of Hays, they told me.'

Andrews wagged his head. 'That ain't good,' he said slowly. 'The raidin' up that way has been mighty bad.'

'You think maybe he . . . ?'

'All I know is what I seen along the lower Solomon. It wasn't purty.'

A new footstep sounded in the yard and Malloy started for the inner door. Nixon stopped him, however, nodding toward the sound. 'That's Helen,' he said, still a little sullen. 'I know her step.'

The girl came in briskly, excitement and anger coloring her cheeks. 'If you didn't eat that lunch yet you'd better come back and have a real supper,' she announced with a determined effort at good humor. 'The excitement seems to be over.'

Malloy shook his head. 'I'd better stay away. No call to let you in for more trouble.'

'There won't be any more,' she said firmly. 'My father has gone out to lodge a complaint against that crazy lieutenant.'

'But won't that take time?'

'Not much. Major Gilmer, an old friend of my father's, is in town. He's in charge of caring for the victims of the Indian raids but he will have authority enough to make that lieutenant hop around.'

'Very well, then,' Malloy agreed. 'If you're sure it won't cause you any more trouble.'

She started for the door without further comment. Andrews grinned at Malloy and remarked, 'Go along. I'll stick it out around the stable. Might see somethin'.'

'And I'll go on over to the office,' Nixon put in.

There was no mistaking his pettishness but no one argued with him. Malloy simply followed the girl across the stable yard and into the darkened kitchen of the restaurant.

'We'll go upstairs,' she said, indicating the stairs. 'Less chance of anyone starting anything.'

'I'm making trouble,' he complained. 'Even your friend Nixon walked out on us. I don't think he was very happy about any part of this show.'

She was making an effort to seem unconcerned as she spoke to him over her shoulder. 'Dave takes things too seriously,' she laughed. 'His job here with the Prairie Express Company is his first real responsibility.'

'But that's not what bothered him tonight.'

They had reached the second floor by that time and she faced him with a smile of challenge on her lips. 'Of course not,' she said quietly. 'Dave's pride was hurt because you succeeded where he looked pretty helpless. He knows that he did not look very heroic—and it bothers him.'

'I can understand,' Malloy said shortly. 'And is there something important between you and Nixon?'

For a moment he wondered if she would take offense at the directness of the question. She colored slightly but replied, 'We are to be married in the spring.'

'My loss,' he murmured. 'And Nixon's carelessness. I can't understand why he is willing to wait so long.'

She changed the subject abruptly, pointing to a table which her mother was busily arranging. 'Am I too curious if I ask why that lieutenant was so alarmed at sight of you tonight? I had a feeling that he took one look at you and forgot all about Dave and me.'

'You're observant,' Malloy said with a smile. 'I guess Walt Loeffler thought I was a ghost—and then he was afraid I wasn't.'

'That's cryptic enough,' she retorted. 'Now that I've been warned to mind my own business I'll help mother with the meal.'

'But I didn't mean it that way. I simply . . .'

'Please don't feel that you have to explain. I did not mean to pry. I was simply struck by his contradictory actions. First he was in a panic, then he attacked boldly enough.'

'I spent years on that problem,' he told her grimly. 'Loeffler's brave enough in some ways but he breaks when he is up against something he doesn't understand. He and I were youngsters together back in Illinois. Walt was the toughest lad in the neighborhood but he never could seem to lick me. I don't know why! he just couldn't. He was always bigger than I but after our first scrap I always knew I could whip him. He knew it too—so I always did. Because he couldn't understand why it happened it worried him.'

He hesitated, suddenly realizing that he was telling this girl things which he had never talked about to anyone, not even Hod

McIntyre. Then he knew that he wanted to tell her, wanted her to know them.

'We enlisted together in 'sixty-one and went down the river with a lot of other uniformed kids who didn't have any idea what war meant. We found out in a hurry—those of us who lived through that first bloody day at Pittsburg Landing. On the second morning of the battle I was sent out to scout in front of our lines. I was a corporal and I was to take two men with me. I chose McIntyre because he was my friend—and Loeffler because I figured he was the best fighter in the company. What I hadn't learned then was that Walt couldn't stand being surprised. He had fought well in the first day's fight, better than most of us, so I was sure dumbfounded at the way he acted when trouble hit us.

'We had been working forward through shattered trees and dead bodies. There didn't seem to be a sign of life anywhere but suddenly something knocked my right leg out from under me and I heard the rattle of muskets from dead ahead. We had walked right into a rebel patrol. The rebels turned tail as soon as they fired on us but Loeffler didn't wait to find that out. He bolted, leaving Mac and me on the ground.'

'The coward.' He could see the sympathy in her eyes and it made him glad that he had unburdened himself.

'I thought Mac was dead. He didn't move. I

had a Minié ball through my leg just above the knee. I yelled to Walt but he kept right on running. There wasn't any more shooting so I tried to crawl back toward our lines. I must have gone about a hundred feet when I fainted. When I woke up again I plugged the hole in my leg with a piece out of my shirt, but when I tried to crawl again the blackness got me in a hurry. I don't know how many times that happened but finally I knew that a rebel charge was going right over me. I remember being surprised when they didn't meet any opposition but the rest of it was just a long bad dream. I woke up next in a rebel field hospital.'

'So he left you and the other man to die or be captured?'

'Exactly. I was plenty sore about it when I had a chance to think it over. There would have been time for all of us to get away if he had stayed to help. I was more bitter than ever a few weeks later when a man from our battalion was brought to the prison where I was held. He told me that Loeffler had been made sergeant for his work in warning of the rebel charge: Walt had gone back with the story that Mac and I had been killed by the advance guard of a rebel division. That was why I didn't hear the rebels meet any gunfire until they were so far beyond me. Our men had fallen back on their supports because of Loeffler's report. The rebels drove forward too far and were wiped out by our counter-attack. Loeffler got the credit for the victory—and I spent the rest of the war in a Texas prison.'

He ate in silence for some moments after that, pausing only at the sound of footsteps near the rear of the building. Helen Temple motioned for him to remain seated. 'It's father coming back,' she murmured. 'I think he's bringing Major Gilmer with him.'

The back door opened and closed quietly, footsteps now sounding on the stairs. Suddenly the girl gave a little cry of dismay. 'That isn't father! It must be . . .'

'Don't move, Malloy!' a harsh voice ordered. 'I'll shoot if you try the least bit of funny business.'

It was Walter Loeffler there at the head of the stairs, a revolver in his hand and the muzzle of a trooper's carbine showing beside him. Malloy's only pleasure in the meeting was the knowledge that the lieutenant was talking thickly. Evidently that punch to the jaw had carried a real sting.

Helen Temple stormed forward, her anger at Loeffler increased by irritation at herself for letting him get in so easily. 'How dare you enter this house?' she demanded. 'You have no right to . . .'

'Take it easy, cutie,' he snapped insolently. 'Don't interfere with an officer in performance of his duty.' His smirk was reflected in his tone. Walter Loeffler was well pleased at the success of his strategy.

'What duty?' Malloy asked ironically. 'Since when has it been duty to make a fool of yourself like this? I thought you had better sense.'

'Shut your mouth!' Loeffler growled. 'I'm running this business.'

'And what a dumb play you made of it! With these witnesses on hand you won't dare to shoot me. Now I'll get arrested and do some talking. Is that smart?'

For a moment it seemed that the lieutenant's rage would overcome his remaining traces of discretion. He took a step forward, his eyes mere slits of venom. 'Don't count on that, Malloy. You won't do any talking. I'll see to that.'

He broke off abruptly as other footsteps sounded at the back door. 'Beckett! Get down there and tell those men to wait outside. They're not to come up unless they hear shooting.'

The soldier hesitated briefly but started toward the stairway. By that time the footsteps were on the stairs and the man came to a quick halt. A florid-faced officer of middle age came into the room, his color deepening at sight of Loeffler's brandished gun.

'Lieutenant!' he barked. 'What's the meaning of this? Have you taken leave of your senses?'

Loeffler's jaw dropped. So did his gun hand. 'Sorry, sir,' he managed to stammer. 'I'm Provost Officer. This man has been . . .'

'I've heard all about it,' Major Gilmer interrupted. 'And from competent witnesses. It's perfectly clear that you have exceeded your authority and disgraced your uniform. You will return to the fort and consider yourself under arrest!'

Malloy tensed himself as he watched Loeffler. For a moment the burly officer had seemed on the point of breaking into open rebellion against the order but then he bowed in elaborate sarcasm. 'Yes, sir,' he said shortly and started for the stairway. There was nothing sarcastic in the glance of hatred which he aimed in Malloy's direction. The old enmity between them would be all the more bitter now that Loeffler had been upbraided before a member of his command.

4

Major Gilmer was not long in getting the whole story. Helen told him in some detail, not omitting the explanation of the background which Malloy had so recently sketched. The officer listened quietly enough in spite of his obvious anger and when the story was over he grinned a little wryly at Malloy.

'You seem to have made friends, young man,' he observed. 'Helen is obviously your champion and so is that lanky rider who rushed me up here so fast.'

'You mean Andrews?' Malloy asked in surprise. 'How did he get into it?'

'I don't know. Temple and I were talking matters over, believing that the row had ended. We had even picked up a couple of soldiers to question. Suddenly this bow-legged cowpoke came galloping in to tell us that Lieutenant Loeffler had come back here for more trouble. We came right over.'

'Lucky you did,' Malloy commented. 'I'm afraid Walt was working himself into a regular crazy rage.'

Gilmer shook his head soberly. 'Naturally, I don't like to see an officer going wrong like that. Was this your first meeting with him since the war?'

'Yes. As a matter of fact it's the first time I've met anyone I knew in the old days.'

'Maybe you'd better let me have the whole story,' Gilmer suggested. 'I'll need to know the facts when I bring charges against the lieutenant.'

Malloy shrugged. 'You don't need to make any fuss on my account. However, if there's any doubt as to my position I might as well explain myself. I was left at loose ends in Texas when the war ended. Instead of trying to work my way north I took a job with one of the new cattle outfits that was catching and branding stray stock. I stayed with them until this spring when I came up with a trail herd to Abilene.'

'And you came here from Abilene?'

'Not right away. I tried to get in touch with my home but found that none of my family was left. There was something of an estate, lucky for me. My father had lived long enough to sell the farm to one of the railroad lines building toward Chicago. I went east to get things settled and decided that it was no place for me. So I came back to Abilene, collected the equipment I had left there and took the next train west.' He grinned slyly at Helen Temple. 'I was still in luck. I picked the train that had the best company on it.'

'And why did you come to Hays City?'

Malloy explained his desire to locate his old friend McIntyre. 'Actually, I want to move on westward but I had a hunch that I might persuade Mac to throw in with me.'

Gilmer shook his head soberly. 'I'm afraid you're doomed to disappointment on that score. Unless my memory serves me badly there was a settler by that name killed in the Solomon raid. He was a war veteran, I'm sure.'

Before Malloy could reply there was a diversion from the street. The rasping voice of Mr. Willie Andrews was making the evening hideous with some of his off-key singing. There was no mistaking the tune this time, even though it was being subjected to all the refined indignities of the Andrews treatment. Malloy had marched behind it too many times when regimental fifes were doing little better than the stooped man was doing now. *The Girl I Left Behind Me* had been sung by soldiers with an infinite variety of lyrics but Malloy felt certain that he was now hearing an original version. At least it was new to him.

'The gals in Texas smile at me.
The Kansas gals are will-in'.
The Injun squaws forget their maws
But Spanish eyes are thrill-in'.

'I got myself a Spanish gal,
A black-eyed senorita.
She weighed about three hundred pounds.
I called her my *chiquita.*

'She gave me half a pint of gin.
I drank it down like water.
She robbed me of my hard-earned tin.
The huzzy hadn't oughter.'

'Our friend seems to like moral ditties,' Malloy commented. 'He was singing another one in the stable.'

'He should sing them all in the stable,' Major Gilmer chuckled. 'But isn't this an odd time to sing?'

Malloy did not care to answer that one. He had his own ideas as to why Andrews was singing. 'Maybe I'd better go out and quell the riot,' he suggested, moving toward the stairs. 'Thanks for the hospitality and please accept my apologies for causing so much trouble. Maybe our next meeting will not be so strenuous.'

The words seemed to be spoken to the entire group but Malloy had a feeling that Helen Temple understood them to be intended for her. It was a pleasant feeling but he did not dwell upon it. He hurried down the stairs and went out into the night, curious to learn why Andrews had decided to lurk outside instead of coming in. Certainly that singing had all the earmarks of a signal that the lanky man wanted to talk with someone in private.

The town was oddly silent as he closed the kitchen door behind him but Andrews' voice came almost immediately. 'That you, Malloy?'

'Right. What's up?'

'I ain't sure. How'd you make out with yore friend?'

Malloy grinned in the darkness. 'No complaint. You got the major around just in time.'

Andrews led him farther from the building. 'I thought I oughta tell yo' about young Nixon,' he whispered. 'When he left here he went right down to the Crossed Swords Saloon—that's where the officers from the fort generally hang out—and I seen him talkin' to that lieutenant.'

'You mean he set Loeffler on my trail?'

'It shore enough looked like it to me. Anyway, the feller headed right back here after Dave give him a earful.'

'But why would Nixon do that?' Malloy wondered perplexedly. 'It doesn't make sense.'

'I pass. All I know is what I seen. The kid was mighty put out about somethin' but I couldn't figure him makin' that kind of a play.'

'Me, either. The boy wasn't too happy because he got cuffed in front of his girl friend but that's no reason for him to play up to the man who slugged him.'

'Unless he figures you're the dangerous one where the gal's concerned,' Andrews suggested bluntly. 'It could be like that, yo' know.'

'So I'd better take a walk down the street,' Malloy said grimly. 'I haven't the least doubt that Walt Loeffler will try to get even with me. If there's going to be another enemy in the offing I want to know about it. Feel like taking an evening stroll?'

'Yo' make it sound right interestin',' Andrews chuckled.

They moved out through the alley, scanning the street carefully before leaving the shadows. It was well that they did. The windows of the Prairie Hotel threw yellow rectangles of light across the board sidewalk and in the gloom just beyond a horseman talked in whispers with a big man who stood close to the gutter.

Malloy reached out to grasp Andrews' arm.

'Hold it,' he whispered. 'There's Loeffler still in town. No use stirring up any more fuss; he'll think I'm trying to rub it in.'

The lieutenant seemed to be doing most of the talking. There was a single comment from the big man on the side-walk and then Loeffler reined his horse toward the middle of the street. Malloy was able to catch his parting remark. 'You're still talking riddles, Mister,' he said, 'but I think I understand. How long will you be in Hays City?'

The big man had to raise his voice to reply as the distance opened between them. 'It's hard to tell,' he said. 'Maybe a week; maybe all winter. I guess we can strike up a deal.' He spoke in oddly clipped syllables which gave the impression that he had rehearsed every word. Malloy remembered the tones even before the big man moved out into the light. It was the frock-coated traveler who had taken charge of the drunk on the train. Evidently he had been making the acquaintance of Walter Loeffler, probably with some definite goal behind the meeting.

Malloy held his position in the darkness until Loeffler disappeared in the direction of the fort. The delay gave him an opportunity to consider this meeting he had just witnessed. Loeffler had been ordered out of town in technical arrest. Yet he had taken time for a quick conference with a man who did not seem to know him very well.

'Something else to keep an eye on,' Malloy murmured as he led the way into the street. 'I'd figure that Walt was so mad that he wouldn't want to think about anything else besides his grudge against me. Does that mean the little confab just now had me for a subject?'

'Seems likely,' Andrews replied. 'We'd better tail that frock-coated jasper just for luck.'

Malloy shook his head as the two men started down the street on the trail of the big man. 'You don't need to get tangled up in this, Andrews. I appreciate the way you rallied around and helped but it isn't your headache.'

'Me,' Andrews remarked cheerfully, 'I like headaches.'

Malloy chuckled and did not argue. It was apparent that this lanky rider had decided to join forces with him. From the very first he had felt a sort of fraternal interest in the stooped man and it seemed certain that the feeling was reciprocated. That suited Malloy. Andrews was obviously a queer sort of bird, but a man might look longer and do worse in finding a partner.

They followed the burly man down the street until he turned in where a burst of yellow light proclaimed a saloon. No other establishment would have been so well lighted.

'Crossed Swords,' Andrews announced. 'It's where the officers from the fort usually hang out.'

'Where Nixon met Loeffler?'

'Right.'

'We'll have a look—through the window first.'

A look was instructive. The frock-coated stranger had gone to the bar and was wrapping long fingers around a bottle which the bartender had set out for him. At his side Nixon held an empty glass. Malloy could not decide whether the pair were old friends or whether this scene represented a mutual introduction. One way or another Nixon was no happier about it than he had been at the stable. His mouth was sullen and he made no attempt to be pleasant even when he held out his glass for the big man to fill.

'Know him?' Andrews asked shortly.

Malloy shook his head. 'Only that he was on the train this afternoon. He seemed pleasant enough then.'

Andrews grunted. 'A real friendly soul, mebbe. First the soljer and now Nixon. He gets around fast.'

'Too friendly to be real, I'm afraid. Shall we bust in and see if he changes his face?'

'What about young Dave?' Andrews asked. 'Was yo' figurin' to put the bee on him?'

'I guess not. I'm curious to see what will happen if we wait and watch. Are you worried about Nixon?'

'Not fer his sake. It's just that I like the

Temples and they seem to set quite some store by the kid.'

'The Temples?' Malloy repeated wonderingly. 'I thought it was just the girl who was interested.' He hoped that his emotions did not reveal themselves in his tone.

Andrews did not seem to notice anything amiss. 'I don't figure he's Helen's choice at all. Judgin' by the few remarks I've heard I figure she's playin' a game for her folks. They want her to marry Dave—so she's plannin' to do it.'

Malloy was suddenly cheerful. 'So we go in and meet our dear friends,' he announced briskly. 'Remember, we aren't mad at anybody.'

They entered the place casually enough but Malloy did not miss a movement of the two men at the bar. Without seeming to look up he noted Nixon's start of surprise. The young man was scared as well as surprised, spilling part of his drink before he gulped it down with a gesture that helped to conceal his agitation. The big man showed no reaction at all for the space of some moments. Then he seemed to recognize Malloy.

'Good evening,' he greeted genially, still clipping off his words in that peculiar manner of his. 'Have you been rescuing any more fair damsels in distress lately?' If he knew Malloy to be the storm center of the evening he did not show it.

Malloy shook his head. 'No drunks,' he said

shortly.

'Too bad,' the big man grinned. 'You handle them so nicely. Have a drink?' He was still completely genial, his wide mouth bearing a careless smile that seemed innocent of any guile. Malloy studied him as he accepted the invitation, seeing some things which he had not noticed on the train. The man was black-browed, clean-shaven and meticulously dressed. At first glance he bore the stamp of the prosperous businessman whose good humor was close to the surface. For Malloy this was no first glance. Consequently he saw something in the green eyes which spoiled the careful pose. This was a man whose joviality was calculated, a cover which hid a cold, ruthless purpose. Whatever might be his reason for making connections with Loeffler and Nixon it was a purpose that would bear careful watching.

'I'm Carlton Brone,' the big man said, still smiling. 'Just in town today, as you know. Got a finger in several pies out this way and I took a trip out to see where I ought to put a few extra dollars to get good returns.'

His manner was expansive even though the declaration was vague. It impressed Dave Nixon. The young man avoided Malloy's glance and introduced himself to Brone, stressing the point that he represented a sizeable organization himself. Malloy named himself and Andrews and they shook hands all around. It would all have been very sociable if there had not been so many crosscurrents of tension between them.

It occurred to Malloy that he was playing the same cautious, waiting game as was Brone. Andrews, on the other hand, almost matched Nixon in his obvious desire to say something that he was not quite ready to say. The result was a rather strained silence.

Then Nixo took the bull by the horns. Forcing a nervous smile he turned to face Malloy. 'Did everything work out all right?' he inquired. 'I suppose it did or you wouldn't be here now.'

There was something comic about the way he seemed to be imitating the easy confidence of Carlton Brone. The comedy lay in the fact that he was not making a go of it. Dave Nixon was anxiously fishing for information—just a little worried about what he might learn.

Malloy let him fish. 'No trouble,' he said tersely.

Nixon fidgeted again, failing to meet Malloy's easy stare. 'I was afraid I might have ruined things,' he said after a moment. 'Lucky nothing came of my blunder.'

'Blunder?' Malloy's eyes were wide and innocent.

Nixon tried to laugh. The effort was not much of a success. 'Yes. I was a little put out because I had not held up my end of the show very well. I thought I might redeem myself by keeping the enemy occupied while you made your plans to get clear. My fine scheme blew up in my face when that lieutenant remembered me. I had to identify myself to avoid being arrested and one of the men nearby tried to help me by mentioning my position as local manager for the Prairie Express. It would have been all right if the fool had stopped there but he had to go ahead and mention my engagement to Helen Temple. That gave the lieutenant ideas. He left me and started up the street. I was afraid he would get back there and make more trouble.'

Malloy refused to commit himself. 'No harm done,' he said cheerfully. He looked suddenly at Brone, trying vainly to catch some sign of expression on the man's politely puzzled features. 'Time to have one on me,' he remarked, 'then I'll have to be moving along.'

They all had another one, chiefly to the accompaniment of nervous chatter from Dave Nixon. Then Malloy and Andrews went back into the dark street. Neither spoke until they were clear of the building, then Malloy asked briskly, 'What bothers you now?'

Andrews grunted. 'Did I show it that much? It's that Brone hombre. I've seen him before.'

'Where?'

'Abilene. A month or so ago.'

'So he didn't just come out this way, eh? Know anything about him?'

‘Nope. I just remember seein’ him around with a bunch o’ fellers what met up with some bad luck not long after that. Most of ’em got shot—or hung.’

‘We progress,’ Malloy murmured. ‘I wonder where Nixon fits?’

5

Malloy indulged himself in the luxury of lying in bed next morning. Even when he was wide awake he remained flat on his back, letting his mind skim restlessly across the panorama of events which had marked his arrival in Hays City. For all that the picture had centered around the revival of his old feud with Walter Loeffler, there were other high lights to be considered, particularly the pleasant ones involving Helen Temple. Somehow he refused to accept her flat statement that she intended to marry Dave Nixon. It was better to ignore that part of the memory.

Mostly, however, he found his thoughts turning to a pair of puzzles. Why were the Temples so concerned over their friendship with Dave Nixon? Where did this man Brone fit into the picture?

It was Brone who was the real riddle. Not only was the man’s personality contradictory, his hard eyes belying his careful smile, but his appearances always seemed to bring up new questions. According to Andrews he had been connected with an outlaw gang at Abilene. On the train he had been a good-natured traveler who had been willing to take care of a quarrelsome drunk. His words with Loeffler had carried an implication of furtiveness. At the Crossed Swords he had been a little too pompous but genial in the extreme.

Perhaps the fat man on the train was the connecting link. Malloy recalled the badge he had felt under the man's coat. It might be that Brone and the fat man were working together as law officers of some sort. That would account for Brone's willingness to assume charge of the troublesome one. It might also account for the obvious falsity of his pose.

The speculations were interrupted by a now familiar sound from outside. Mr. Willie Andrews was coming through the alley from the direction of the railroad tracks, offering a new song to the bright, warm morning. Malloy lay still and smiled. Having decided to like Andrews he wondered whether he also had to like that kind of singing.

This time the tune was *The Son of a Gambolier*, another song which had suffered mistreatment from the soldiers of both armies. Andrews, of course, had his own peculiar way of torturing it.

'I'm a parson's son from Lexington,
I warble in the choir.
I help to pass collection plates
To pay my rev'rend sire.
I never cuss and never smoke,
A moral life I've led.
I'm a parson's son from Lexington;
I might as well be dead.'

It seemed to settle one point. Not all of the Andrews songs pointed a moral.

A half hour had passed and Malloy was splashing briskly in the cracked washbasin when a knock came at the door.

'Come in,' he called, reaching for a towel.

It was Andrews. The lanky one grinned apologetically and folded his ungainly length into a rickety chair. 'Been scoutin',' he announced abruptly. 'Town seems peaceful.'

Malloy mopped his head and chuckled. 'Too bad. Nobody to fight with today, I guess.'

'Mebbe not. Yore lieutenant's still out at the fort. The major seems to be gone, too.'

There was a pause and then Andrews added, 'Nixon chewed the fat with Brone 'til well after midnight. Dunno what about. Dave's over at the restaurant now.'

Malloy ignored any possible implications in the final remark. 'I suppose you didn't pick up any hint as to what Brone's business is?'

'Nope. Yo' interested?'

'Just curious. I'm not planning to stay in Hays so I don't care a whole lot about local matters. It's just that the man puzzles me.'

'Me, too. Yo' sure yo' never seen him before?'

'Only on the train.'

Andrews shook his head. 'Funny. He kept lookin' at yo' as though he had some funny ideas. Kinda like he knew yo' and was gettin' a heap o' fun outa knowin'.'

'Sorry I can't do as well for him—not that I would be likely to get much fun out of it. I just don't like the man, even though I don't know why.'

A slow grin twisted the lanky man's wrinkles. 'Fer a soft-spoken waddy yo' sure do have a way o' makin' enemies, Malloy. Yo' ain't hardly hit town before yo' got four gents itchin' fer yore scalp.'

'Four? I didn't figure I had any enemy except Loeffler.'

'No? How about that fat feller?'

'All right. He bears me a grudge—if he remembers me.'

'And Dave Nixon? Yo' didn't fall fer his spiel last night, did yo'? He's workin' up a right fair hate on yo' because he's afraid yo're tryin' to steal his gal.'

Malloy did not reply.

'And Brone makes four. Don't ask me why. I don't know. I just figure he's a bad hombre and yo're in his black books. He'll rawhide yo' if he can—and smile like a chessy-cat while he's doin' it

Malloy tried to laugh it off. 'You're a pessimist, my friend. It must be that you're soured in your soul because of that noise you make when you sing. The idea sounds reasonable, anyway.'

* * *

Five minutes later they went in to the little restaurant where so much swift drama had been packed into such a small slice of the previous evening. Dave Nixon sat at one of the tables, talking across the room to Helen Temple as he finished his breakfast. The girl was at the cash desk, dressed for the street and consulting some notes as though getting ready to go shopping. There were no other persons in the place.

She looked up as the two men entered, her quick smile in direct contrast to Nixon's poorly concealed scowl. There was an exchange of greetings and Helen asked a sober question. 'Did you know that Major Gilmer was called away suddenly? It means he won't be able to follow up last night's business.'

Malloy shrugged. 'I don't mind. I wasn't too keen on having the army handle my personal affairs anyway.'

'But the lieutenant may try to take it out on you.'

'Let him. I'll certainly be ready. Remember that I have a score to settle with him, too.'

Nixon climbed to his feet a little stiffly. 'Ready to go, my dear?' he asked. 'It's time I was at the office.'

She did not seem to notice his manner. 'Right away,' she said quietly. Then, with a smile at Malloy, 'On my way to do the marketing. I'll be seeing you around town, I suppose?'

'No doubt about it,' he assured her.

Spots of color came into her cheeks as she met his eyes but she changed the subject rapidly, nodding toward the kitchen door. 'There's father. He'll take care of you.'

Temple came forward with a grin. He was wearing duck pants and an undershirt, the apron around his rotund middle giving him a professional appearance. 'Mornin',' he greeted. 'Looks like ham 'n' eggs is about all we've got. That do?'

Both men voiced agreement and he disappeared without another word. Malloy had expected at least a comment on the events of the night but Temple seemed to have something else on his mind, something which occupied his thoughts quite pleasantly.

They could hear him shouting from the kitchen, however, and Mrs. Temple appeared promptly, more than making up for her husband's silence. Under her prompting they rehashed every point which Malloy was willing to discuss and it quickly became apparent that Nixon had done some talking this morning. Not about Loeffler, evidently, but certainly about Brone.

Suddenly Mrs. Temple changed the topic. 'Major Gilmer left a message for you, Mr. Malloy. Did my husband give it to you?'

'No.'

'It's about that friend you came here to find. The major checked up on it and it's like he said last night. He thinks there can be no doubt but what the man you're seeking was killed by the Cheyennes last month.'

Malloy had been prepared for it to a degree but the news was still hard to take. He nodded quietly but said nothing. In such cases there was nothing to say.

Mrs. Temple tried to keep the talk going. 'We know how you feel. We've seen a lot of this sort of thing. Does it break up your plans so much?'

He shook his head. 'I'm afraid my plans are pretty vague. At least in detail. I'm hoping to work out into the eastern foothills of the Rockies and plant myself in some of that rolling grasslands that I've heard talk about.'

'Not this fall,' she protested. 'It's coming winter and the Indians are raiding all through that country. I know; it's the section we're expecting to settle in and we don't dare go yet.'

He concealed his quick satisfaction at the news. 'I'm not ready to go yet. I'll probably use the winter to study some maps and get an outfit together. Spring will be time enough for me.'

'Maybe the border will be clear by that time. There's talk of a winter war to clear the country for all time.'

He had lost his feeling of strangeness that he should confide in Mrs. Temple. Now they were fellow members of the great army of trail blazers, both interested in the problem of getting the way cleared.

'I'm not optimistic about a winter war,' he told her. 'Too much politics in army camps. Officers will grab the jobs that seem to offer chance of promotion but they'll shirk anything that means hard work and discomfort. A winter campaign will be all hardship and no glory. I can't count on it for much after what I've seen of the army, particularly this social club army that the officers have developed out here.'

The ham and eggs came in then. Andrews took an appreciative look but wagged his head doubtfully at Malloy's words. 'I used to figure the army just about the way yo' do, Sid,' he drawled. 'But I shore changed my mind after I spent two weeks holed up on that island in the Arickaree. It was mighty comfortin' to see a line o' blue coats comin' across the plains. I reckon I wouldn't be divin' into these ham and eggs now if there hadn't been some reg'lars around.'

'I'm prejudiced,' Malloy admitted with a short laugh. 'But I've seen army life from a number of angles and I don't like any of them. First it was the Illinois volunteers with everybody wanting to be some kind of an officer or get some kind of a medal. Nobody had any idea what war was like or how it ought to be fought—or why they were fighting. That was the worst part. When you see men being killed and mangled all around you it helps to know why you're there. Not many of us knew in 'sixty-one.'

'I kin see that,' Andrews admitted with his mouth full. 'And the ignorance wasn't all on yore side o' the line. I was with the Texas troops and I never did figure out why. The whole shootin' match seemed mighty dam' silly after the spit and polish wore off. I didn't own any slaves and I didn't want to see the Union busted up, but there I was.'

'That's my point exactly,' Malloy said. 'The man to fight Indians ought to be the man who knows what Indian troubles mean, not a New York down-and-outer taking orders from a professional parader with one eye on a polishing rag and the other on the officers' seniority list.'

'I still liked the looks o' them darky troopers of the Tenth when they rode up to Beecher's Island,' Andrews said stubbornly. 'Mebbe they didn't know why they was there but we was sure glad they was!'

'But it was your men who fought the battle,' Malloy argued. 'Men who knew why Indians had to be fought; not men making a career of formal bloodshed. I still can't make myself like the idea of the army as I see it out here. It's just an officers' club with enlisted men as cheap servants. Whether they can fight or not doesn't alter the fact that it seems like something out of middle Europe.'

Mrs. Temple laughed a little uneasily. 'Maybe you would prefer our state militia,' she remarked. 'We have a recruiting officer in town, Captain Farnsworth. He's trying to get men for a state regiment to work with the regulars.'

Malloy glanced at her wonderingly. 'You make it sound as though you're trying to get us in the army. I'm not having any, thank you.'

The lady protested. 'I didn't mean you particularly. I just meant . . .'

'No matter,' Malloy said with a smile. 'But let's talk about something more pleasant. Colorado, for example. Did you say you intended to settle out there?'

Temple came in from the kitchen in time to answer the question. 'You bet we do,' he said with enthusiasm. 'We've got a real proposition with the Kansas Pacific people.'

'I thought yo' liked the eatin' house business,' Andrews said with a puzzled frown. 'How come yo're goin' into railroadin'?'

Mrs. Temple took over the explanation.

'The railroad wants to set up a restaurant stop somewhere west of Sheridan. It looks like we're going to get the contract to run the place for them. It'll be pretty big, I think.'

'When do you take over?' Malloy asked.

'It isn't settled yet—and of course the railroad line won't be built until next summer. However, Dave Nixon has been working for us, using his influence on friends back east. For a while he didn't seem to be making much headway but last night he learned something important. It appears that there's a railroad man in town. He's keeping pretty quiet about his business but Dave got friendly with him and they seem to understand each other. He practically promised that we will get the contract.'

'A man named Brone?' Malloy asked quietly.

'That's right. You know him?'

'I've met him.'

Neither of the Temples seemed to notice his reserve or the quick look he exchanged with Andrews. They vied with each other in their enthusiastic descriptions of the place they saw in their dreams, both of them too excited to notice Malloy's preoccupation. Not that the mention of Brone was enough to account for the younger man's abstraction. Out of the corner of his eye he had seen Dave Nixon entering the recruiting office across the street. It seemed like an odd move for a man who had been so anxious to reach his own office.

Presently Malloy found an opportunity to ask a question. 'What happens to Nixon and his freighting business when the railroad runs its lines west?'

Temple was expansive. 'All of them big companies are hooked up together. It'll be like it was here. This was the freighters' main depot when it was the end of the rail line. Now they're runnin' stuff west of Sheridan but they still keep this office busy, mostly with army work to the south. Rails may handle main line business but the wagons will still do the branch work.'

'It keeps Dave mighty busy,' Mrs. Temple put in. 'We thought he was a little young for the job when his folks put him out here but it looks like he's doing mighty well for himself.'

Malloy grinned amiably. It was not too pleasant to hear Nixon being lauded by these people but it was no time to throw cold water. 'It looks like everybody but me expects to get rich out of this new move westward.'

'But you have your plans,' Mrs. Temple objected.

'Not big ones. I'm afraid I'm not especially ambitious. Among my other foolish ideas I have a hunch that a man ought to spend some of his time enjoying the world instead of trying to get rich so he can burn himself out trying to get richer. That valley ranch will satisfy me. If I can have some peace I won't ask riches.'

'Peace,' Mrs. Temple repeated slowly. 'I wonder if it isn't too much to expect. We never seem to have peace out here.'

'We can always hope,' Malloy replied.

He had seen Nixon leaving the recruiting office, a smile on his face. Evidently that young man had more strings to his bow than appeared on the surface. Certainly he had impressed the Temples. But was his act genuine?

He paid the bill for himself and Andrews, the two men losing no time in leaving the restaurant. The day was warming up and they stood silent in the sunshine for a moment before starting up the street. Malloy was still trying to make up his mind about several bits of information which had come his way. Mostly he wondered about a possible connection between Dave Nixon and Brone.

Finally he nodded silently to Andrews and the pair of them started across the alley entrance. They had taken only a few strides, however, when a voice hailed them from across the street. 'Andrews! Malloy! Come over here a minute, will you?'

Malloy glanced around in astonishment and saw that the voice came from the militia officer he had previously noticed. The man was standing in the door of his office, beckoning to them.

'That's dam' funny,' Andrews muttered. 'How does he know our names?'

'Nixon was just in there,' Malloy informed him. 'I wonder if our bright young man isn't using this as a scheme to get us out of town. And if he is, why is he?'

'Wanta go over?' Andrews asked grimly.

'Sure. Maybe we'll learn something.'

6

The militia officer greeted them warmly and ushered them in to his somewhat cramped corner of the store. He was a big-bodied man who looked too heavy for his long, spindly legs, his multiple chins and massive head adding to the top-heavy effect. The smile was genial, however, and he went right to the point.

'I'm Captain Farnsworth, men, of the Nineteenth Kansas Cavalry. There's a matter I would like to talk over with you if you have a few minutes to spare. I've been hearing about the excitement of last evening and it struck me that you might be just the type I need. There's also the matter of Andrews' service with Forsyth's scouts.'

'If it's enlistment you want to discuss,' Malloy interrupted, 'you'll be wasting your time. My plans are such that I can't commit myself for any period of service. To be quite frank with you, I'm not interested anyway.'

He watched the officer as he spoke,

wondering how much the man knew and what part he actually played in this strange tangle. Certainly that blunt announcement ought to make the captain put all his cards on the table.

Farnsworth kept his good-humored smile. 'You get ahead of me, Malloy. Or are you Andrews?'

'I'm Malloy.'

'Right. I had no thought of trying to enlist you men in the regiment. I would like to offer you jobs as civilian scouts on the same terms offered by the Federal forces. We propose to operate in conjunction with the Seventh Cavalry this winter and we should have the same sort of scout service that they have. Would such a proposition be more interesting to you?'

Malloy hesitated. Employment as a scout was something he had not considered. Moreover, it would not be as formal as enlistment. 'Under what sort of contract?' he demanded. 'How long a time, I mean.'

'Monthly basis,' Farnsworth replied. 'We can't make any estimate as to how long the campaign will last, but you would be guaranteed three months' pay. In return you guarantee that you will serve at least that long. After three months you will be hired from month to month.'

Andrews was interested now, Malloy could see. For himself there was something to be said for the offer. He had an idle winter in prospect. This job would not only give him some employment but it might take him into the very country he wanted to explore. Then he recalled his suspicions of Nixon. If this whole setup was a game to get him out of Hays City and away from Helen Temple he didn't want any part of it.

'It's a generous offer, Captain,' he said politely. 'However, I'd like to talk it over with Andrews before I give you an answer. Then, too, I'll have to see my way clear in other ways.'

'No hurry,' Farnsworth replied. 'I'll hold the offer open for a couple of days.'

They left the recruiting office and went over to Malloy's room. By that time Andrews had lost his brief enthusiasm. 'Stick with me,' he advised. 'They tell me a feller named Pepoon has got command of Forsyth's old outfit, the colonel hisself bein' still in bad shape from the wounds he got on the Arickaree. The word is they're comin' here to Fort Hays. Them boys know their Injun fightin'.'

'Who said I wanted any fighting?' Malloy asked with a smile. 'I've spent most of the morning explaining how I just want peace and now I've got two people trying to work me into some kind of military organization. Or is it three? I still think Nixon was behind this offer.'

'Yo' kin still make it two,' Andrews retorted. 'I was just talkin'.'

For the balance of the day Malloy was busy with other matters. He established credit with a local banker, arranging to draw on his St. Louis funds for purchase of equipment. He checked with the land office and was convinced that it had indeed been Hod McIntyre who had died in the Solomon raid. The rest of the time he spent locating and buying equipment for his westward move. Better to get things ready now instead of waiting for the spring rush.

The only flaw in the otherwise peaceful afternoon was the fact that at supper time he did not see Helen Temple. The little restaurant was busy but she did not appear. Her parents greeted him warmly enough but there was no opportunity for conversation. Nixon came in just as Malloy was finishing his meal and the young man barely nodded. Evidently he had made up his mind that he was not going to be friendly.

Consequently it was something of a surprise next morning to be hailed in jovial fashion by that same young man. Malloy had just stepped out of the hotel door when he heard his name called. Nixon was coming along the sidewalk in company with Carlton Brone and the fat man who had caused the trouble on the train.

Nixon introduced the pudgy man with a show of pomposity. 'Malloy, meet Thatcher Vance. You know Brone, don't you?'

Vance extended a pudgy hand, studying

Malloy with a frown on his round face. 'Seems like I've seen you somewhere before,' he commented. 'Been around here long?'

'Not long,' Malloy said evenly. 'You probably mistake me for somebody else; lots of people as ugly as me.'

Brone laughed significantly. He seemed to think it a fine joke that Vance should have failed to place Malloy. Then he jerked his head toward the end of the street. 'Looks like an escort coming in to meet the train,' he remarked, his words snapping oddly as he clipped them off in that peculiar manner of his. 'I wonder if we'll meet anybody we know?'

The question sounded entirely innocent but Malloy was not deceived. For some unaccountable reason Brone was passing a broad hint. Malloy ignored it. 'On the train, you mean?' he asked.

Brone laughed. 'No. We know who's coming on the train. General Custer is due, coming to take command for this campaign they're planning. We'll see some action when he gets into the saddle.'

Malloy did not reply. Not only had he been with the Army of the West but he had spent most of the war in a rebel prison. Thus he had little knowledge of a cavalry commander who had made his reputation in Virginia. It was the pudgy Vance who bristled at the remark. 'What kind of action?' he snapped. 'Just a lot of useless fuss over his wife, his six horses, his dozen hound dogs, his four servants and ten wagonloads of baggage. The redskins can turn the country inside out while Custer's holding a parade or taking half his command out on a buffalo hunt or some such nonsense.'

The violence of the statement astonished Malloy, even though it fitted in pretty well with his own opinion of the peacetime army's style. Brone, however, smiled indulgently. 'The old war cry,' he commented. 'There seems to be no middle ground on Custer. We either think he's a wonder or we hate him. I'll grant that he's a show-off, Vance, but he's a good fighter at the same time. Sheridan wasn't long in picking him when he saw what kind of a fight this would be. If there had been anybody as good on the army rolls Sheridan wouldn't have gone to so much trouble to get Custer reinstated.'

'Rats!' the fat man scoffed. 'What did Custer ever do that was so good? The Cheyennes made a monkey of him last summer. All he did was ride his horses and his men to death. Then he ordered men shot for leaving the force when they were half crazy with thirst. Fine! Splendid discipline and all that sort of thing. So what does he do when the command needs him most? He left them! No wonder they court-martialed him and kicked him out of the army. I don't see why Sheridan wanted him back.'

'Because he's a fighter,' Brone repeated,

apparently amused at the fat man's vehemence.

'Sure. But what kind? Hell for leather and no judgment. We wouldn't have the border in a stew now if Custer and old Windbag Hancock hadn't stirred up a lot of peaceful Indians last summer. He's likely to make a bigger blunder if they give him a chance.'

Brone shook him off with a show of good nature, turning to Malloy. 'We're setting up a small game of draw poker at the Crossed Swords,' he said significantly. 'Want to come along and show us some fine points of the game?'

'No, thanks,' Malloy replied. 'I'm trying to clean up a few chores around town and I'll be too busy for poker during the next few days.'

'Maybe later,' the big man grinned. 'I'll try to get along on what money I can get out of the express company and brother Vance.' He laughed a little too loudly as he winked at Vance and Nixon. Somehow Malloy felt that Carlton Brone liked his jokes subtle; the real humor lay in the fact that he was being serious in his statement—and laughing at his two companions because they thought he was joking. Malloy decided that he was not a good man for a greenhorn to buck in a poker game.

General George Armstrong Custer arrived in Hays City with almost as much fanfare and baggage as Thatcher Vance had predicted. There was a brief flurry of action in town and then he rode out with his escort toward Fort Hays. Malloy caught only a glimpse of him, a glimpse of a tall, lean man whose long hair and mustache helped to hide the youthfulness of his countenance. There was an air of nervous energy about him and a hint of instability in his eyes. Rumors of his wild rages seemed to bear out the impression that he was a man who might depend on emotion for his decisions.

Conversation in town seemed to run pretty much along the lines of the Brone-Vance argument. There seemed to be no neutral observer on the subject of General Custer. He was either a brilliant hero or an arrant jackass.

Hays City's military interest was heightened that evening when news came in of another skirmish to the northwest. There had been no serious clash since Forsyth's fight on the Arickaree but now the Indians had struck again. General Carr with a squadron of the Tenth Cavalry escorting him to Fort Wallace had been chased almost to the gates of the post by a strong band of Cheyennes, Arapaho and Sioux. A punitive force of the Fifth Cavalry, reinforced by Pepoon's Scouts, had driven the Indians far to the northwest of the post, burning several villages and inflicting some casualties.

Next day another war report came in and this time the events were less spectacular but closer. A train had been derailed only a few miles west of Hays, the Indians having cut off the ends of enough ties so that a rail had dropped and put the engine on the ground. Even with the advent of cold weather the Indians were continuing to raid. Apparently they knew that a full scale war was in the offing and they were determined to inflict as much damage as possible on the whites before snow could hamper their raids.

Malloy shrugged off the excitement of the townfolks, refusing to discuss the Indian troubles at any length with anyone. Captain Farnsworth met him once along the street and pressed him for an answer but Malloy declined to accept the offer. He was a little surprised when the militia officer assured him that the proposition would still be kept open.

It was not more than an hour later that another courier came in with news, this time from the south where General Sully had been campaigning from a temporary post which he had dubbed Camp Supply. Driven into a frenzy by the harassing tactics of the Indians around him he had waged a two weeks' campaign which had been a model of futility. He had been outmaneuvered and outfought by inferior numbers, returning to his base to blame Major Elliot, the officer in command of the eleven troops of the Seventh Cavalry which had been the main force of the command.

'We'll be hearin' from Cap'n Farnsworth again, I reckon,' Willie Andrews remarked that evening. 'They'll be anxious to make a stab at gettin' square with the redskins and it's a fair bet that they'll push matters a bit.'

'The news is just the sort of thing I've been complaining about,' Malloy said. 'Parade ground tactics don't have any place in the kind of fight this one has to be. We won't win any wars with the Indians until we fight them their way—and we won't do that until we have officers who know something besides the right way to wear a dress uniform and which fork to use when the commander invites them to dinner. We'll have to have a commander with more sense than to send out infantry against mounted Indians, for one thing.'

'I'll wait for Forsyth's outfit to show up in these parts,' Andrews insisted. 'That's the outfit to fight Injuns.'

'You're still not talking to me,' Malloy retorted.

The following day brought no significant development in the puzzling local situation. Andrews reported that Walter Loeffler had been in town to see Carlton Brone but Malloy did not see either man. For that matter he did not meet Helen Temple or Nixon either. He took his meals at the hotel, passing up the better food of the little restaurant in order that he might settle a few things in his own mind before seeing the girl again.

It was well along in the evening when Andrews came into the Prairie Hotel. The lanky one seemed disturbed but his greeting was cryptic. 'Want to amble down the street a piece?' he asked. 'There's somethin' yo' might want to take a squint at.'

Malloy did not press him. He went along promptly, certain that his new friend must have something on his mind that would bear investigation. Andrews maintained his silence, leading the way to the barroom of the Crossed Swords. Then Malloy understood. A poker game was in progress there, a game in which Dave Nixon, Brone, Vance and two other men played silent, watchful poker. Malloy glanced briefly at the two strangers, then went with Andrews to the bar, turning presently to glance back and study the situation.

Young Nixon looked worried in spite of the alcoholic slackness in his expression. He was keeping one eye on his cards and the other on his stack of chips as though he could not understand why his stake had dwindled so much. Thatcher Vance was drunk again but this time he did not seem belligerent. Just unhappy. His fat jowls and extra chins were quivering and red in the lamplight and his eyes were too far closed for much expression to show. However, he was pawing his cards with a nervousness that was eloquent.

Carlton Brone looked up as Malloy entered the room. The big man's eyes were keen. Either he had not been drinking or he could carry his liquor far better than Nixon or Vance. He was intent on the game and he knew what he was doing, something which could not be said for the other two. The pair of strangers seemed sober enough but neither of them acted particularly alert.

A glance at the chips indicated nothing startling but Malloy knew better than to judge a man's luck by the size of the pile in front of him. He would have bet that both Nixon and Vance had bought several times. Nixon's expression and Vance's nervous fingers were fair evidence of that.

'Evening, Malloy,' Brone greeted with his best smile. 'Want to sit in—or haven't you finished that other business yet?'

Lurking behind the smiling question was a vague implication which Malloy could not quite understand. The big man seemed to be accepting him into his confidence as though they had a secret in common. It surprised him—and left him a little resentful. 'Not tonight,' he said quietly. 'I'll wait until you've finished your proposed conquest of these other gentlemen.'

The big man frowned. Apparently his joke of the earlier meeting was no longer funny. Vance scowled, Nixon murmured angrily beneath his breath and one of the strangers swung in his chair to ask, 'What yuh mean by that, brother?'

He was a lean, hard-looking man of about Malloy's size and build. Expressionless eyes stared from beneath shaggy brows and Malloy thought of a gun fighter he had known in Texas. Malloy met the level stare, his own face calm. 'I wasn't talking to you, brother,' he retorted, matching the man's phrasing without imitating the tone.

There was a split second of almost crackling silence before Brone's voice came sharply and with authority. 'He's all right, Windy. It's just a joke between us. Get back to the game.'

The man's sullen obedience gave Malloy another item to put in his collection for rainy day thoughts. This fellow Brone was no casual gambler; he would be a good man to watch.

Joining Andrews he turned his back deliberately on the poker game. They lingered over a drink and when Malloy turned around again he was in time to see Dave Nixon bringing out his wallet. The young man's lips were tight now. Ugly realization had driven some of the fog from his brain.

'One more stack,' he said thickly. 'And then I'm done for the night.'

'I'm done already,' Vance growled. 'Deal me out.'

He rose unsteadily and waddled toward the bar, his round face redder than ever and his coat flapping open so that Malloy caught a glimpse of the badge he had felt before. 'Cleaned,' the fat man grumbled, half to himself. 'Every damned penny!' Then he stared belligerently at Malloy. 'Dammit, man!' he said suddenly. 'I swear I've seen you somewhere before.'

Malloy shook his head. 'No dice.' He turned abruptly away and wandered toward the poker table. Sooner or later Vance would remember and then there would be a bit of fuss. No use encouraging the fool to make a jackass of himself until it was necessary.

As he turned toward the table he caught a flicker of movement which aroused memories. That artillery lad from Ohio had used the trick when the prisoners played poker for rations. So that was Brone's game? Holdout cards. The big man had not been indulging in idle talk when he proposed to take the Vance and Nixon bankrolls; he was doing it with all the efficiency of the frontier gambler. Maybe that was why he had been so willing to take charge of Vance on the train; he had smelled sucker money.

Malloy hesitated at the sight, shrugging almost unconsciously as he caught Brone's look. Again that indefinable something passed between them. Brone knew that his crooked deal had been seen and for some reason he did not care. He even winked at Malloy before going on with the fixed game.

Again Malloy felt a resentment at the way he was being accepted by this genial crook. It had been gratifying to have a feeling that he could exchange silent understanding with Helen Temple but it was irritating to find himself in the same sort of strange relationship with Carlton Brone. He was tempted to step in and expose the game but common sense restrained him. Interfering in other people's business, however crooked, was not done in this part of the country. No one would thank him for it, not even Vance and Nixon. Certainly he could expect only trouble from the man Brone had called Windy. Anyway, it was none of his business. He owed no debt of kindness to either Vance or Nixon.

His sudden anger cooled but he knew better than to stay around and risk more trouble. Without waiting to speak even to Willie Andrews he turned and went out into the night.

7

Malloy was in a quandary. He felt that he should tell the Temples what he suspected, yet he realized that they probably would not believe him. They wanted to believe in Brone because he represented a way for them to achieve their goal in the world; it would be hard to make them understand that the man was a fraud. Still they ought to know. They might be throwing away good opportunities while they waited for Brone and Nixon to make good on their promises.

He considered it thoughtfully as he watched

a string of Nixon's wagons come into town and make camp near the railroad tracks. Thus preoccupied he almost missed seeing something which interested him. Carlton Brone was just coming out of the militia office. Certainly the man was not proposing to join the Nineteenth Kansas. Malloy laughed shortly to himself, suddenly sure of his own conclusions. First Nixon and now Brone. That would mean another offer from Farnsworth before many hours. Why were they so anxious to get him out of Hays City?

Deep in his own perplexed thoughts he almost bumped into Helen Temple as he walked up the street. She met him with a smile but he knew at once that something was troubling her.

'You're a stranger,' she accused, pleasantly enough. 'Didn't the Temples feed you well enough to keep you as a satisfied customer?'

He tried to keep it on the banter level. 'Too good. I've lived on hard-tack and salt pork for so long that I can't trust my stomach with too many civilized victuals. I might get the gout.'

The joke did not go. She was direct. 'You have avoided us,' she said quietly. 'Is there a reason?'

'Nothing either of us can help,' he replied.

Maybe she read part of the reason in his eyes. At any rate she flushed a little, steadying her voice carefully as she went on. 'I was hoping I would see you. I wanted to ask your advice.'

Neither of them seemed to think it strange that she should thus apply to a comparative stranger. It was the most natural thing in the world for her to do—and because it was he was both glad and troubled. 'About an apple pie recipe?' he asked, still striving for the lighter note.

'About Dave Nixon,' she said evenly. 'I'm afraid he's riding for a fall. He's been gambling for the past couple of evenings with that man Brone. Dave can't risk the kind of money that Brone plays for.'

Malloy did not reply. There was no point in denying her assumption that Brone was wealthy. It was beside the point anyway. There was an equally good reason why Nixon could not afford to gamble with the man.

'I wondered if you had a suggestion,' she added almost wistfully. 'I have a feeling that something is very wrong with this whole situation, yet I can't put my finger on the flaw.'

He shook his head thoughtfully, trying to decide whether he should explain his own partly formed suspicions. It would have been pleasant to feel that he could confide in her but somehow he could not convince himself that such was the case. 'I simply can't tell Nixon how to run his own affairs,' he said shortly.

'You mean you won't help me?' The angles were back in her face as she met his eyes.

'Not where Nixon is concerned. That's none of my business. If you're asking for advice, however, I'll give you some. Find a way of making direct contact with the train folks about that eating house business.'

Her eyes widened. 'Why?' she demanded.

'Isn't it fairly clear how I feel about it? Take a trip east to headquarters. Go yourself if you can; you'll be the best agent your folks could send.'

He had expected anything from anger to ridicule when he made the statement. To his surprise she nodded with quiet understanding. 'You don't believe in Brone, do you?'

'No.' It was better not to add that he had no more confidence in Dave Nixon.

She glanced around cautiously before asking, 'Then you think Nixon is being cheated at cards?'

'I do.'

'But you refused to help—even against a crook.'

He studied her for a moment, then decided to be frank. 'Suppose I make myself clear. I meant all I said to you the other day on the train. I thought I was about to make up for all those years of ill fortune. Then I saw you meet Nixon and knew that I had met you too late. Within another day I had changed my opinion once more. I don't believe you love him. I think you like him well enough to play up to him for the sake of your parents' ambitions—

but you don't love him. So I don't propose to do a thing on his behalf.'

An inscrutable smile played about her lips. 'You're quite complimentary—in a rather hard fashion,' she said after a moment. 'Would you really have Dave injured by a gambler rather than help him?'

'Why not? He means nothing to me except trouble. If you haven't guessed it by this time I'll tell you that I'm pretty much in love with you. It wouldn't cause me much grief to see Nixon shown up for the stuffed shirt I'm beginning to think him. If at the same time I get some kind of a line on this mysterious Brone character I'll be doubly pleased. Does that explain why I won't help Nixon?'

'All too well,' she replied, turning away.

That night he went deliberately to the Crossed Swords, his intentions not entirely clear even to himself. The old restraint was gone, however, and he was reckless but tight-lipped as he entered the place to find Thatcher Vance and Carlton Brone sitting idly at a table. The fat man was genial again and apparently in funds, a point which brought another question to Malloy's mind. Did the man have some sort of drawing account which permitted him to recoup his poker losses or had he entered into some kind of deal with Brone?

'Business seems to be about cleaned up, gents,' he announced quietly as he crossed the room to join them. 'I figure it's my night to fill some inside straights. Would there be a game on the docket?'

Brone gave him that curious, half-lidded smile. 'Some men are incurable optimists on the subject of inside straights,' he remarked. 'Have a drink? Nixon and one of his wagon bosses will be along pretty soon. You'll make as good a fifth as we're likely to find—even if we can't hope that you'll be exactly profitable.'

Malloy tried to make sense of that remark and failed. He met Brone's quizzical glance and remarked idly, 'Nixon, eh? Aren't you being a bit rough on the boy? Even with the stakes you've been playing you've taken him for quite a sum.'

It was a dangerous remark and he knew it. Brone was not the man to accept such open criticism and he was big enough and ruthless enough to carry his resentment to extremes. Malloy waited for the eruption he had fully expected but the big man kept his perplexing smile. 'Maybe we'll have to ease up on him,' he said shortly.

Vance seemed agitated by the turn of the conversation. He had come to his feet at Malloy's remark and now he started toward an inner door. 'I'll be back pretty soon,' he said hurriedly.

As soon as he was out of the room Brone looked back at Malloy. 'Were you planning to draw cards on the Nixon deal?' he asked quietly. The words were calm enough but the clipped quality of his enunciation was more pronounced than usual. This time Malloy could understand his man a little easier. Brone was conveying a cautious warning. The mystery was why he was being so cautious about it.

'Nixon's not my meat,' Malloy said, still sparring for some sort of move he could interpret. 'I just thought we should understand each other before we start the game. I've played before with gents who had clever ways of keeping a few extra cards on tap.'

Again he knew that he was asking for trouble but once more the big man refused to take fire. 'I thought you were on to me,' Brone said casually. 'Who did you know? Any old pals of mine?'

Malloy grinned, partly at the man's nonchalance and partly because it helped to conceal his own nervousness. 'Not likely,' he said, falling back on the truth. 'This lad was a gunner in an Ohio battery. We were fellow boarders in a rebel prison and we had a deck of cards. He could make them sit up and talk—and since none of us had much for him to win he told us his secrets.' He did not add that the Ohio artilleryman had found an apt pupil in a certain Illinois foot-slogger. That was a point which it might be well to keep as a hole card.

'I understand,' Brone said, his smile indicating that he did not believe a word of it.

'What's your proposition?'

'None.'

Brone's smile faded. 'I don't think I understand you as well as I thought I did,' he said flatly. 'You wouldn't be trying to warn me off, would you?' For the first time those clipped tones carried a ring which could have but one interpretation. The big man's careful politeness was a thin veneer covering a menacing danger.

'Nothing like that,' Malloy assured him, still composed. 'In the first place it would be a silly thing to do—and in the second place I'm not interested in Nixon's financial success. I'm just in the mood for a quiet poker game. I wondered if I was going to get it.'

Brone's quick laugh contained unquestionable relief. 'You're a queer bird, Malloy,' he chuckled. 'I don't savvy your play at all but for tonight it's poker with none of the trimmings. Satisfactory?'

'Satisfactory.'

Dave Nixon came in then, accompanied by a squat, wide-shouldered man whose right cheek bulged with an oversized quid of tobacco. Malloy wondered briefly whether Nixon had become suspicious and was bringing a strong arm lieutenant with him. Certainly the burly ape looked ugly enough, from short, bowed legs to low forehead and close-cropped red hair. Even his grin displayed crooked teeth which snarled through what he evidently thought was a smile of greeting.

Nixon's manner, however, was cordial. If he had any suspicions of his poker companions he was keeping them under cover much better than Malloy believed he could. He introduced the gorilla as Bull Grimby, interrupting the acknowledgments with an impatient, 'Where's Vance? When do we start?'

Vance answered the first part of the question for himself, appearing at the rear door to throw a peculiar glance at Malloy. Brone contented himself with replying to the other half of the query. 'We were just waiting for you,' he said carelessly. 'Our mutual friend Malloy has finally broken down and consented to expose his wealth to our designs. Maybe a little fresh money in the game will change your luck.'

'It's about time,' Nixon said. In spite of the lightness of his tone it was evident that he was laboring under a strain. Malloy decided that the young man was risking more than mere money in this game tonight.

Brone motioned to chairs and a grimy waiter came forward to bring cards and chips. 'Just a sociable game,' he told Malloy and Grimby. 'Mostly we bet two-bits at a time. Dollar limit. Nobody gets hurt.'

Malloy nodded agreement, still puzzled. A man like Carlton Brone did not fit into a game of this caliber. Not only that, but the game had been going on for several nights now. That usually meant a hiking up of the limit but in this case it had not happened. Why was a smooth crook like Brone doing his act for peanuts? Was he playing for something bigger to come or had he simply gauged the suckers' ability to pay?

Malloy found no answer to his question in the first hour of play. To all intents and purposes this was just the sociable game Brone had named it. The pots were mostly small and so were the winning hands, little cash having changed hands. With an hour of dull play behind them Brone was a few dollars in the hole, Nixon was about as much ahead and the other two men were nearly equal partners in financing Malloy's tiny profit. No one had made any move that seemed at all off color.

Then Nixon became restless. A little success seemed to remind him that he had a lot of money to get back. He started to force the betting, capitalizing on several hands that were just good enough to win over weak opposition. Then he drove the bets savagely upward as two successive straights and a small flush beat fair cards in other hands. The others became careful in the face of the winning streak and Nixon won twice without being called. His poorly concealed smile indicated that he had succeeded with a pair of good bluffs. By that time he was a substantial winner, the only winner in the game.

Now would come the test, Malloy knew. He

had been watching Brone as Nixon's streak continued and it was apparent that the big man was repenting his promise to play the game without frills. It was Brone's deal and something in the way the big man kept his eyes averted told Malloy that it was not to be an honest deal. Brone had remained straight as long as he could stand it.

The gambler's fingers were nimble but Malloy knew what to expect. As soon as the cards were dealt he threw his own hand to the table, not even glancing at it. 'I spent my money for education this time,' he said without any particular emphasis. 'Ante money can be cheap learning.'

Only then did Brone look up. There was a challenging humor in his sardonic eyes and Malloy knew that the man was laughing quietly. It was almost startling to recognize the cool effrontery of it all. Brone was putting on a crooked deal, knowing that Malloy was aware of the fact. And he was defying Malloy to do anything about it. Maybe that remark about getting an education was not too far amiss. He was certainly learning something about the character of Carlton Brone. The man had nerve and he was in no way backward about welching on his agreements, even to a man he considered as a fellow thief.

8

For a moment Malloy was tempted to blast the gambler's cockiness but he decided that it would be a foolish move. Even if he could prove any accusation he might make he would accomplish little or nothing. Better to wait until he knew a few more things. If this was only a small part of Carlton Brone's crooked game it would be worth a little forbearance to find out what bigger business was behind this strangely picayune gambling.

Brone watched until Malloy's shrug gave him answer. Then he grinned in open triumph and went on with the deal. Vance opened and Grimby immediately threw in his cards. Nixon raised the opener and Brone bumped it another four bits. Vance stayed, grumbling, and Nixon added another raise. It was still peanuts but it had to mean something.

'You're too tough, I'm afraid,' Brone told Vance. 'I call. How many cards do you want?'

Vance took one, Nixon two and Brone three. After that the pattern was one Malloy could have called almost in detail. Vance dropped out as soon as Nixon's limit bet indicated that he felt confident. After that it was a sort of slugging match with Brone and Nixon hammering raises at each other. The big man put on a good appearance of being a little sorry for himself as he met Nixon's final raise. 'I thought I was better than average,' he said with a wry smile. 'Now it looks like I bit off more than I can chew. How big are you?'

Nixon grinned broadly and threw down three eights and a pair of queens. 'I picked up the queens to go with my trips,' he commented with open satisfaction.

'Almost enough,' Brone said quietly, his voice a little more restrained than usual. 'I picked up one jack and a pair of fours to go with my original pair of jacks. Talk about dumb luck!'

'Jacks over fours?' Nixon echoed, his voice changing abruptly. 'That beats . . .'

'Your luck failed you,' Brone chuckled, raking in the pot. 'First time there's been a full house in the game tonight and we get two of them together. Tough.'

Nixon swallowed hard but managed a smile. 'Somehow it always seems to go like that with me.'

'Stick around,' Malloy said aimlessly. 'Maybe the luck will bounce back.' This time he was the one who avoided the look of inquiry tossed at him.

Vance took the next pot with a single pair and it was Malloy's deal. He could feel Brone's eyes upon him but he dealt without looking up. That was one advantage of having watched Brone so carefully. He had a pretty good idea of the big man's ability—and of his limits.

Brone was pretty smooth with his own neat bag of tricks but it wasn't such a big bag. A certain Ohio artilleryman could have made a monkey of him. Malloy felt pretty certain that Brone would not detect the false move in the deal, even though he was evidently suspicious of something.

There was a brief interval of silence as each man studied his cards, then a flurry of opening bets and raises which more than matched the hand Brone had dealt. Malloy looked up for the first time, caught Brone's eyes still upon him, and shrugged a little. 'I seem to have taken care of everybody except myself,' he complained, tossing his cards to the middle of the table.

The words and the gesture seemed to satisfy Brone. He tossed in another raise only to have it hiked another notch by both Grimby and Nixon. Vance went along, still complaining.

Grimby took one card while each of the others drew two. Then Grimby cursed and dropped out. Nixon studied his hand, opened with a limit bet and was promptly raised by Brone. Vance added another dollar and the betting went around three times with each man raising. Then Vance called and hung on while the other two continued to hammer each other. Finally it was Brone who called, this time without benefit of any comments. His swift look at the expressionless Malloy indicated that his suspicions had come back to him without any happiness whatsoever.

Vance also called, with a sigh of relief, and the three of them turned their cards down almost at the same moment. The fat man cursed bitterly when he saw that his spade flush was a poor third. Brone had another full house, aces over sixes, but Nixon laughed delightedly as he spread out four fives and a deuce.

Malloy sat back, watching Brone narrowly. 'I think that's enough education for me tonight. Hands like that make me dizzy.'

Brone swallowed hard but said nothing. None of the others seemed inclined to comment either and Malloy climbed to his feet, elaborately careless but not missing the significant nod which Brone had directed to someone in the far corner of the room. He pretended to be interested only in locating his hat but it was not difficult to swing around and see that the only occupants of that corner were the two hard-looking characters who had been in the previous game. So Brone was calling his henchmen into action? What were they supposed to do?

He permitted himself no illusions in the matter. Carlton Brone was not the man to balk at a little violence and the dark street of Hays City was almost void of pedestrians this dark night. It would not pay to put himself in an exposed position.

He drifted lazily out of the Crossed Swords

but as soon as he was clear of the door his demeanor changed. A half dozen swift strides took him to the corner of the building and he took cover behind it just as Brone's lieutenants came out.

He could hear the flurry of bootheels on the planks of the sidewalk, then silence as they halted in some confusion. 'Which way did he go?' the dumpy man's voice growled.

'Musta lit out fer the hotel,' Windy retorted. 'Come on. We gotta grab him before he gits to where somebody might see us.'

'Gonna shoot?' the other asked.

'Shore. Carl ain't givin' us the high sign less he means business.'

The footsteps came on again and Malloy had a moment to be sorry that he was not carrying a weapon. Then the pair were hurrying past his hiding place and he stepped out behind them, his voice taking on some of the incisiveness of a sharp blade on a frosty morning. 'Hold up there! Hands high!'

Both men skidded to abrupt halts. Before either could recover sufficiently to turn around, Malloy had reached out and snaked the dumpy man's gun out of its holster. With his free hand he took a firm grip on the fellow's collar, holding him as a shield while he snapped another order at the hesitant Windy.

'Don't start for iron, Windy,' he warned. 'Brone won't love you if you're all full of holes.'

'What's goin' on?' the man whined. 'You can't . . .'

'Up with those hands! Quick.'

The man seemed to make up his mind. The hands went up and he fell back on the whining tone once more. 'What's the idea o' holdin' us up this way? We're jest a . . .'

'Don't try to be cute! Turn around and back toward me —with your hands up there where I can see them. Fast now!'

He released his grip on the dumpy man's coat collar, slapped efficiently for a possible second gun, then quickly relieved Windy of his .44. 'Now head back toward the door,' he ordered. 'We'll go back and report to the boss.'

Neither man offered any protest but Malloy was aware that Windy had slipped some sort of sign to his companion. It wasn't like either of them to submit so tamely. They had been bowled over by the swiftness of it all but now they were planning something, probably a break which would come when they reached the interior of the Crossed Swords. Brone might be depended upon for assistance there.

'Don't be too cocky about it,' Malloy warned, as though he had read their thoughts. 'The first shot hits Windy if anything goes wrong.' He reached out to take the man's collar as he had previously grabbed the dumpy one.

'We ain't . . .' Windy began.

'Shut up. You ain't anything just now. Open

the door, squatty! Careful now. That's right. Hold it there.'

He released Windy, retrieved the extra gun from his coat pocket and met the astonished glances of the men at the poker table. 'Your little playmates, Brone,' he said quietly. 'You shouldn't let them run the streets at this hour of the night. Something might happen to them—and to you if you ever try that stunt again!'

With the words his foot came up, poised momentarily against the seat of Windy's breeches, and heaved. Windy was catapulted howling into the poker game and Malloy backed out into the darkness.

No one followed him. He waited briefly at the door but no one even approached it. Above the uproar from within there was but one sound distinguishable. It was the fat man's voice shouting, 'Now I know that rascal!'

Back in his room at the Prairie Hotel Malloy spent a couple of hours in serious thought. The evening had been enlightening in a number of ways but it had scarcely been helpful. No longer was there any doubt as to the character of Carlton Brone. The man was a double-crosser, a smooth card sharp and a deliberate, cool killer. He had not hesitated to order the death of the man who had dared to oppose him, masking his deadliness all the while under that smooth smile of his. How did such a character fit in with the other factors?

Why was he playing a game for relatively small stakes?

Even more important at the moment was the question of what Brone would do next. Certainly he would not take Malloy's challenge without offering some counter move. Hays City was not going to be a very safe place in the future.

To add to the complication there was the fact that Thatcher Vance had remembered Malloy as the man who had handled him so roughly on the train. If Vance and Brone were not already allies, they would soon strike up an alliance.

* * *

The following morning dawned clear and cold, a real chill of winter in the air although October was not yet gone. Malloy had his breakfast at the hotel, regretting the decision which kept him from enjoying the superior food of the Temples' restaurant. Then he went back to his room before going out into the street, buckling on the gun belt which he had not worn since coming to Hays City. As he stepped out of the front door of the hotel he knew that he had made a good move. Carlton Brone was coming out of the militia headquarters across the street. Malloy waited tensely, watching the man for an offensive action, but to his surprise Brone came straight toward him, a broad grin on his face.

'You're tough, my friend,' Brone greeted easily. 'I think we had better get together. No point in battling each other when we can throw a lot of weight jointly.'

'You didn't seem to feel that way about it last night,' Malloy replied coolly.

Brone laughed aloud. There did not seem to be any limit to the man's good nature when he wanted to put on the appearance of being a genial companion. 'I was a little hasty,' he said without any trace of rancor. 'You got under my skin with that act of yours and I called the move too soon. Want to show me your deal some time?'

'Which one do you mean?' Malloy asked dryly. 'The one where Nixon gets four fives or the other deal where I draw myself a pair of six-guns?'

'They're both good,' Brone said, his smile still easy although his eyes no longer met Malloy's. 'But what I meant was the card trick.'

There was nothing in his tone which would have led a casual observer to think that only a few hours before he had ordered the murder of the man to whom he was now talking so pleasantly. Malloy was not a casual observer. He had been studying Carlton Brone long enough to be sure that the man was all the more deadly for his complete geniality. Now he was having trouble keeping the smile in place—and he was not sure enough of his own emotional control to expose his own eyes.

Somehow the realization brought a sense of triumph to Malloy. Even though he knew that he was treading on dangerous ground it was satisfying to know that he had broken into the outer defenses of this self-sufficient outlaw. He even decided to spar for a moment. 'I might break down and discuss the matter,' he conceded. 'Of course it's not ethical in the profession but among friends I guess it will be all right.'

Brone's smile suddenly showed a trace of malicious triumph. 'Among friends, eh? I thought I had you figured right but that Ohio artilleryman talk sounded almost true. Now it runs in my mind that there was a smooth gentleman who used to work the Mississippi steamboats. His name was Carey, I believe. From all accounts he was a dead ringer for you, looks, nerve, clever fingers and everything. You never heard of him, I suppose?'

Malloy ignored the heavy sarcasm even though he realized that this conversation was explaining many things. Brone had mistaken him for Carey at their first meeting. That was why he had played the game as he had. Maybe it indicated that he was honest in his present offer of alliance. Maybe.

'That's right,' Malloy said, still expressionless. 'I never heard of your friend.'

'Too bad,' Brone chuckled, evidently

satisfied with his own guess. 'I heard that he ran into a streak of bad luck. He stabbed a man in St. Louis and had to retire from the river. Now he's supposed to be somewhere out here in Kansas, disguised as a cowboy or a settler.'

'Sounds like quite a gent,' Malloy said. 'Sorry I never had the pleasure of meeting him.'

Brone chuckled, all good humor again even to the eyes. 'If that's the way you want it I won't argue,' he agreed. 'We'll go around again sometime.'

Malloy watched him cruise along down the street and something in the big man's attitude troubled him anew. Most of his questions were at least partly explained now but he still did not know what Brone's real business was. Nor did he understand why Brone was so happy about fastening the Carey name on him. Still there was a clear warning in the situation; when Carlton Brone was pleased with himself someone needed to take additional precautions.

While he was pondering the matter Willie Andrews came out of the Temples' restaurant and hailed him. 'Heard the news from the fort?' he asked.

'What news?'

'Sounds like the big show is about to roll up the curtain. General Sheridan's movin' out fer Camp Supply to meet Custer. The talk is that they're plannin' to hit the redskins jest as soon as the snow flies.'

'In the snow? That sounds awkward.'

'It sounds plumb smart when yo' stop to think about it. Jest like that trooper said the other night, when reg'lars go after Cheyennes it's a danged pore show. The Injuns jest light out and the troopers can't ketch 'em. Now the game is to let the reds git snowed up in a winter camp where they can't run away. That'll learn 'em a thing or two!'

'You make it sound good. Are you working up enthusiasm to join the Scouts?'

Andrews seemed disturbed. 'I can't git no word of 'em or I would,' he replied. 'One report is that they're to go south with Sheridan and another is that they're goin' to be busted up. Nobody seems to know 'zackly where they are.'

Malloy chuckled. 'I guess you're due to fall,' he said. 'You won't be happy you're with 'em again.'

They walked down the street together, discussing the proposed campaign against the Indians, and went in to the post office. Andrews was not looking for any mail and he turned idly aside while Malloy went to the wicket, scanning the bulletin board with its faded notices. It was only when Malloy had asked vainly for mail that he looked over Willie's shoulder and noticed the name in large capitals on a 'Wanted' circular. The name was Thomas Carey.

It reminded him of the cryptic remarks of Carlton Brone so he read the circular carefully. This man Carey was evidently the crook and card sharper Brone had named him, his latest exploit being the cold-blooded murder of a victim who objected to being fleeced. The important part, however, was that the description of the fugitive fitted Malloy exactly.

Andrews apparently had not noticed the coincidence. He turned, grinned amiably at Malloy, and led the way out to the street again. There was no time to mention the circular, for as they opened the door they came face to face with Carlton Brone. The big man eyed Malloy quizzically, nodding a little toward the post office. 'Did you see the poster?' he asked. 'Not a bad description—even if it isn't very flattering.'

Malloy chose to answer the question which appeared on Andrews' bony face. 'Don't mind Brone, Willie. He simply has a peculiar idea that I'm a confidence man named Carey. Rather ridiculous when you think that he's going by a description that might fit hundreds of men.'

Brone's careful smile took on a shade of acerbity. 'Not many of the hundreds could also deal so expertly,' he retorted. 'But that's not why I came across to speak to you. I just saw Thatcher Vance studying that same circular over at the hotel. I knew he was interested in you but I didn't think he was that smart.'

'Is this intended as a friendly warning?'

'You might take it as that. Vance is some kind of a detective, a Pinkerton man, I believe.'

Malloy studied him frankly. 'For a man who had such unfriendly designs on me last night you certainly have become helpful all at once. Am I supposed to believe you've had a change of heart?'

Again he was baffled by the big man's self-control. 'Suit yourself,' Brone laughed. 'You can believe me or not—but it might get awkward around here if Vance lets his ideas run away with him.' Then he turned abruptly and went into the post office.

9

Malloy told his story to Andrews as they walked back toward the Prairie Hotel. Willie made no comment until the various angles of the situation had been explained. Then he grunted, 'Carey, huh? Are yo'?'

'No. There doesn't seem to be anything except a similarity of descriptions that would account for the mistake—but that could be enough to cause trouble. Too many dead-or-alive reward hunters around.'

'Yo' think Brone's givin' yo' a good steer on this?'

'It looks like it—although I can't see why. But then I don't understand him anyway.'

Andrews looked troubled. 'If I was yo' I'd git outa this town fer a spell. It wouldn't be like runnin' away from anything; it'd jest be givin' troubles a chance to aim theirselves at the right parties. Yo're in a heluva mess that ain't no business of yon'n at all.'

Before Malloy could reply a voice hailed them from the far side of the street. It was Captain Farnsworth once more and the militia officer seemed even more anxious to talk than had been the case before. Malloy grinned at his companion as they headed across toward him. 'Maybe this is a hunch,' he remarked, half seriously. 'Joining the volunteers would get me out of town while things settle down.'

Willie shook his head. 'Wonder if he's got a new offer?'

Malloy's smile faded. With all the seriousness in the world he whispered, 'Do you suppose he wants you to sing for the general?'

Willie snorted audibly. 'Better forget the funny stuff and make up yore mind to git outa town—either this way or some other one.'

Captain Farnsworth greeted them cordially but did not mention business until he was seated behind his makeshift desk, looking as important as possible. Then he put on a show of abruptness, covering, Malloy thought, an uneasiness which the man could not quite conceal.

'I need two civilian scouts right away,' he snapped. 'It's a matter of pride that we have someone to represent the Nineteenth Kansas in General Sheridan's column. In the emergency I'm prepared to offer an additional twenty-five dollars a month. Rest of the offer the same as it was before. Will you take it?'

Both men hesitated. Willie was balancing the prospect of extra pay against his sentimental memories of the scout detachment. Malloy was silent for entirely different reasons. For one thing, he could not believe that the state regiment would offer extra pay for so flimsy a reason. With suspicion already established in his mind he connected the offer with Brone's earlier call upon Farnsworth. But what was the reason behind it all? It did not seem to match Brone's apparently friendly warning.

'There's one condition,' Farnsworth added. 'You would have to get out of town at once. General Sheridan is to leave Fort Hays for the theatre of operations either today or to-morrow. You're worth the extra pay to us only if you can be on hand to accompany that movement.'

Andrews glanced at Malloy and seemed to make up his mind, evidently more concerned with his companion's needs than with his own desires. 'I'll sign on,' he said shortly.

Malloy gave up. 'I think you're stampeding me, Willie,' he chuckled dryly, 'but I guess it's the best thing to do. Count me in.'

'Good.' Farnsworth was more pleased than the circumstances seemed to warrant. 'Be back here within the hour and ready to ride. I'll prepare the necessary contracts while you're collecting your outfits. As civilians, of course, you will not be able to draw upon government commissary officers.'

'Fair enough,' Malloy said, turning to follow Andrews out to the street. Then he added as they crossed toward the hotel, 'I suppose I'm a complete fool ever to get near an army again but I'd just as soon have Indians shooting at me as I would drunken detectives. You at least know where you stand with Indians.'

He secured his belongings from the hotel room and went deliberately across the alley instead of heading back toward the stable. There was one thing which had to be done before he left town. It could be postponed no longer.

At that hour of the morning the little restaurant had few patrons. Mrs. Temple was at the cash desk and her eyes clouded as she saw Malloy. It was easy to know that something was bothering her but he affected not to notice. 'Is your daughter around?' he inquired. 'I'm leaving town today and I wanted to say goodbye.'

'You, too?' she asked, her glance still

puzzled. 'I wish somebody would explain a few things to me. First we have Dave Nixon busting in here like a crazy man in the middle of the night, then Helen goes East on the morning train without explaining a thing to any of us—and now you are going away. What's it all about?'

He gave her a disarming smile. 'Nothing very mysterious in my case,' he replied. 'Andrews and I are going to Fort Hays as civilian scouts with the Nineteenth Kansas. It's just a winter job as far as I'm concerned. What was wrong with Nixon?'

'I'm sure I couldn't tell. He came here with a lot of crazy talk about somebody cheating him out of his money. Then, without making a bit of sense, he shut up and wouldn't say any more about it except that he had been drinking too much.'

'And did Helen decide to go east after that?'

'I suppose so. She hadn't said anything about it before then.'

'You'd better trust her, Mrs. Temple,' Malloy said quietly. 'I think that young lady knows what she's doing.'

* * *

On the short ride to Fort Hays Malloy told Andrews the full account of his suspicions about Carlton Brone. It was better than allowing his mind to rest on the encouraging fact that Helen Temple had gone East. Maybe she was following his advice and maybe she wasn't. No use getting optimistic.

Andrews was a little impatient about Brone. 'Forget him,' he advised. 'Yo're outa town now; who cares what the jasper's game is?'

'I'm stubborn,' Malloy said with a little laugh. 'It irks me to suspect that he had a hand in getting me out of Hays City. I'm still trying to see a sensible connection between his visit to Farnsworth's office and all that talk about Carey.'

* * *

The matter might have been clarified had he been able to overhear the conversation in Brone's room at the Crossed Swords. Brone was there, together with the squatty man and Windy.

'I guess we're rid of Carey at last,' Brone said with open satisfaction. 'It cost me a little money but I persuaded Farnsworth to handle the job. Cheap enough when I think how he rawhided you poor fools. I couldn't afford to have him around any longer; he could ruin a lot of things.'

The other men squirmed uneasily at the criticism but Windy found courage to ask, 'How'd yuh work it?'

'Easy enough. I let him know that our pet detective was on his trail, then I passed the word to Farnsworth that Malloy is something extra special in the scouting business. As a patriotic citizen I was willing to put up a little extra money to be certain that our state heroes had the best of scouting service. Farnsworth swallowed that and then Malloy—or Carey—swallowed it from Farnsworth. Anyway he's gone, taking that bowlegged old pilgrim with him.'

Windy grimaced appreciatively. 'Glad I'm on yore side, Brone. Yuh shore figure things out. Now, when do we grab them wagons?'

* * *

Malloy found ample opportunity to renew his complaints against military red tape. After being hurried off to Fort Hays on short notice he and Andrews spent just fifteen days at the post in almost complete idleness. Their only orders had been to join the escort going south with General Sheridan so there was nothing to do until the march began. That was a matter of some delay, the reports having been entirely false with respect to the commander's presence at the fort. He had not yet arrived there.

On the third day of their enforced idleness a squadron was ordered out on the trail of Indians who had attacked ammunition wagons coming east from Fort Wallace, but neither Malloy nor Andrews could get permission to go along. The regulars made it clear that they had no use for civilians attached to a militia outfit. Hence neither man had an opportunity to read signs which might have hinted at the truth, that the raid was not the work of Indians at all. It was not until much later that they heard a scout remark on the fact that Indians had neither the organization nor the enterprise to run off with such bulky loot. Likewise it was not until they were far to the south that Malloy learned that the wagons had belonged to Nixon's company.

Meanwhile Andrews had been using the opportunity to overcome certain deficiencies in equipment. Ingratiating himself with various supply sergeants, he managed to secure extra blankets, new weapons and a plentiful supply of ammunition.

'I just hope none of the officers gets to asking questions,' Malloy told him with a smile. 'We'd have a hard time explaining how a couple of old sod busters happen to carry these new Officers' Models.'

Andrews just grinned. 'Big improvement over them old hawglegs, ain't they? Next I'll git us a couple o' Spencer carbines. Then we'll be ready fer a good scrap.'

Pepoon's Scouts arrived at the fort ten days after Andrews and Malloy. They had been diverted on the trail of the ammunition wagons and it was from them that Malloy heard the first hint as to the real nature of the raid. Someone was stealing ammunition on a large scale, probably to sell to the Indians.

Having no orders to the contrary, Malloy and Andrews moved in with the irregulars and for the time being could breathe more easily with their dubiously acquired equipment. Most of the scouts were similarly outfitted and Major Pepoon was too smart an officer to ask questions. Like his unfortunate predecessor, Colonel Forsyth, he realized that he was little more than a liaison officer for this rough crowd and he left the detailed work of command to Sharp Grover, Chief of Scouts. Past experience had shown the arrangement to be a good one and Pepoon did not propose to risk the efficiency of his company for the sake of formality.

With Andrews occupied in renewing old acquaintances Malloy seized the opportunity to make a trip into Hays City. It had been irritating to remain there so close to town and still seem so far away. Regardless of the risk he might be taking he wanted to see Helen Temple again, so in the cold dusk he saddled up quietly and slipped out on the trail toward town.

His choice of evening proved unfortunate. The streets seemed deserted when he walked his mount toward the center of the little town but he was hailed sharply as he dismounted in front of the restaurant. Too late he realized that he had not even glanced toward the recruiting office. Someone over there had seen him outlined against the restaurant lights and had recognized him. In the darkness he could not make out the identity of the person who had called but he had a feeling that the voice was that of Captain Farnsworth.

Annoyed and more than a little uneasy he crossed the street, keeping his pony with him. Farnsworth spoke again, the strain apparent in his tone. 'Come in here a minute, will you, Malloy?' he asked. 'We're having a little trouble.'

Behind him were the familiar forms of Brone and Vance. Trouble was right. Malloy tied his mount with a slip knot and made sure that his gun was loose in its holster as he moved toward the door. There was no mistaking the tension in the room as Farnsworth opened with a question that was merely his way of postponing the real issue. 'What are you doing in town, Malloy?' he demanded. 'This isn't . . .'

'More of the army's eternal dilly-dallying,' Malloy cut in. 'General Sheridan hasn't even showed up at the fort yet.'

Farnsworth nodded hastily. 'So I heard. But that is not why I wanted to see you. Charges have been made that you are an escaped murderer. Naturally, I . . .'

'Sure. I see your point and I know the line. Our fat friend here claims I'm a lad named Carey. Is that it?' He saw that Vance was tense behind the desk while Brone lounged easily in a chair, his broad face openly amused.

It was Vance who replied, a pudgy hand hovering close to his coat buttons. 'Going to confess, hey?' he inquired with a sneer that helped cover his uneasiness.

'Don't be a fool!' Malloy snapped. 'I'm not Carey and you don't have any good reason to think I am. You'd just like a good excuse to get even with a man who didn't appreciate your drunken antics! Keep your hand away from that pocket!'

'Let's not have any trouble,' Farnsworth pleaded. 'I simply want to . . .'

'And he probably pulled that wagon robbery,' Vance interrupted angrily. 'I demand that he be arrested right away.'

'On what grounds?' Malloy inquired. 'I'm not Carey—and if you would stay sober long enough to check your facts you'd know it. I didn't pull any wagon robbery; I can prove where I was at the time of the only robbery I've heard about. Use your head for something besides a rack for all those extra chins!'

'Talk's cheap!' the fat man retorted. 'I still think you're Carey.'

He turned as though to walk away, quickly converting the motion into a surprisingly agile draw of a concealed derringer. 'Up with . . .'

Malloy had not been fooled. Vance found himself staring into the muzzle of an Officer's Model Colt, his own weapon still only half drawn. It was almost comic to see the way his hand and jaw drooped in unison.

'Too bad I'm not really Carey,' Malloy said dryly. 'I'd probably rid the world of you right now. Drop the popgun. Now turn around and walk over toward the wall. Hurry!'

Brone grinned amiably from his chair. 'Is that the way you handled Mike and Windy?' he asked.

Malloy gave him a swift glance, finding time to marvel at the man's insolent nerve. With violence threatening all around him he could make jokes about the murder attempt he had himself ordered. 'Something like this,' Malloy replied, picking up the fallen derringer. 'Now, fatty, start for the door and keep going. I might get to thinking I'm Carey.'

Brone kept his grin but followed Vance. 'You're a tough hombre—Malloy,' he said dryly.

Farnsworth made an effort to reestablish his lost dignity when the pair had departed. 'I don't like this, Malloy,' he said brusquely. 'I can't have gunplay in my office and I can't have my men dodging the law.'

'Sorry about the first,' Malloy replied. 'And the second part is not true.'

'I believe you. But there will be trouble if you stay in town. As your superior officer I order you to return to Fort Hays and remain there until you can carry out your previous instructions.'

Malloy suppressed a smile at the man's nervous formality. 'Very well, sir.'

Farnsworth's relief, was apparent. He even ventured a smile. 'And don't stop to visit our friends across the street. Vance will be perfectly capable of ambushing you if you wait around long enough for him to make plans and get a weapon.' There could be no question as to the soundness of the advice. Vance would certainly try some new move and there was a strong probability that Brone would help him. The big man's show of friendliness meant nothing.

'Back to the fort.' Malloy agreed grimly. 'But all I hope is that our friend Vance actually finds this Carey jasper some day. It might sober him up.'

He was not in a happy frame of mind as he headed back across the prairie toward the fort. There was too much running away in this new program. Sooner or later he would have to face the issue and prove himself. Meanwhile he had to live under the strain of not knowing where he stood with a number of different people. Nixon, Brone and Vance each offered a threat to his happiness and he could not quite understand what any of them proposed to do. The Loeffler situation was even worse. He had to remain idle on that point, not knowing where his old enemy was nor what he might have planned to do.

It left him a little bitter that he should be

leaving every one of those problems at a loose end. Troubles didn't clear themselves by being left alone.

10

General Sheridan arrived at Fort Hays on the following day and events began to take on a livelier tempo. The commander-in-chief was not a big man nor an impressive looking one but his crisp decisiveness matched his remarkable record. Sheridan cut red tape with the best of them, accomplishing real results while other officers floundered in formalities. Malloy decided that serving under him might have its advantages.

Despatches coming in from the south hinted at trouble in the camps along the Arkansas and Cimarron so the commander issued prompt orders for the march south. Evidently there was bad blood between Sully and Custer while the troops were on the verge of mutiny and the Indians continued to raid fortified posts with the greatest boldness.

Barracks gossip was more definite and, as so frequently happens, was quite accurate. Custer had found Sully's command in a sorry state and he had set out to establish organization and discipline. In spite of his harshness he was making good soldiers out of the demoralized

Seventh Cavalry's personnel but he was outraging Sully at the same time. There was a bitter dispute between them as to the real command, their ranks being equal, but Custer had ignored Sully to assume command of the entire force. Obviously Sheridan was going to have some family feuds to settle before he could launch the Seventh Cavalry on any such ambitious campaign as was rumored.

Malloy heard it all with a sort of detached impatience. Bickering between officers always filled him with disgust but now he was too intent upon his own troubles to think much about it. Each day he expected some move on the part of Thatcher Vance but three days passed and no word came from Hays City. Apparently Farnsworth had managed to convince the fat man of his mistake. Still it was not a pleasant mess to leave behind.

On the fifteenth of November trumpets aroused the fort to a wet, predawn blackness that was ominous and depressing. Rain had fallen all during the night, a driving northerly storm in which sleet had mingled with cascades of water to turn the prairie into a veritable quagmire. Wagons which had been loaded the previous afternoon were sunk into the mud until it required extra teams of mules to get them started on the trail southward. Dawn broke drearily through a freezing mist, carrying a chill to the marrows of men's bones as successive detachments filed out of the fort.

Pepoon's scouts were leading the way, followed by the long supply train.

Malloy and Andrews watched as the regulars and the baggage wagons departed, then they crossed to where Sheridan's staff officers were preparing to take their places in the two ambulances which had been provided for them.

'Civilian scouts Malloy and Andrews, sir,' Malloy reported to a dejected looking staff captain. 'Our only orders are to accompany this force. Where do you want us?'

The captain studied them in some surprise. 'What regiment?' he asked brusquely.

'The Nineteenth Kansas Volunteers.'

'No orders about you, I'm sure. I don't believe the adjutant even knows you're here.'

'That suits us,' Malloy said with a smile.

Surprisingly enough, the officer chuckled his agreement. 'Maybe it's just as well,' he conceded. 'The general likes to have scouts near at hand when he's traveling through new country. I'd suggest that you bring up the rear and keep within hailing distance of the commander's ambulance. That is no order, you understand; I'm simply making a suggestion.'

He turned away before any more questions could be asked. Malloy caught Willie's eye and they rode toward the north side of the parade ground, keeping well out of the way of the last units leaving the fort. 'Real army stuff,' Malloy growled. 'Nobody knows anything unless it's down in general orders. We're lucky we ran across an officer with some imagination. If we'd struck some of these brass button beauties we might have held up the whole war while somebody spent hours finding out about us.'

They waited for an hour, sitting their broncs in the freezing mist while the commander's official family made ready to depart. The wagon train was out of sight and hearing when a muddy rider came into the fort from the direction of Hays City. Andrews hailed him briskly. 'Howdy, bud. Nice mornin' to go out ridin', hey?'

The man seemed to recognize him. 'Hi, Willie,' he greeted. 'Where do I find the provost?'

Andrews pointed to the proper building. 'Why? Goin' to give yerself up?'

The rider grinned. 'Got to see if anybody from here was ramblin' around in the rain last night. A man name of Vance —fat feller—got a bullet between the ribs sometime after dark. Found him lyin' in the mud just this side o' town this mornin'. Deaden'n Santa Anna.'

He moved on toward the provost's office, leaving Malloy and Andrews to exchange significant glances. Willie was the one who found his tongue. 'Well, what d'ye know!' he exclaimed. Malloy did not reply.

The staff ambulances jolted into motion

then, lurching toward the muddy trail which the baggage wagons had made. Andrews and Malloy followed silently. Another mystery was being left behind.

Malloy found plenty of time to think about the death of Thatcher Vance. There was nothing to do but follow the ambulances on the dreary march. They crossed the Smoky Hill at ten o'clock and reached Big Timbers Creek at noon, having covered twenty miles in spite of conditions. There they came up with a squadron of troopers who had been left behind to serve as escort to the staff. They had extra horses with them and the officers took to the saddle for the afternoon, most of them thoroughly weary of riding in the ambulances.

The afternoon was even worse than the morning had been. It rained steadily and the mud became deeper and stickier. There wasn't any doubt that the staff was now far behind the rest of the column, so it was not at all comforting to see the occasional savages who hovered on the nearby prairie swells. It would be quite a coup for the Indians to wipe out the headquarters detachment before it could even make contact with the main body of troops.

The need for vigilance helped Malloy to keep his thoughts from the troubles he had left behind him. With Andrews he ranged the country daringly, trying to lure the Indians into making a false move, but nothing happened until it was nearly dark. Then another body of troopers drifted back to strengthen the escort and a couple of sharp charges dispersed the lurking Indians.

A chill camp was made on the north fork of the Powder, men and officers trying vainly to sleep without benefit of campfires. There was no wood and everything was wet, so it was a case of everybody getting such rest as was possible in the freezing blankets. After a forty mile battle with mud and rain it was not a pleasant camp.

Andrews and Malloy took full advantage of their peculiar status. Not being regularly attached to the command they drew no assignment when picket duty was passed out, and so were able to adopt cowpuncher methods of keeping warm in spite of the snowfall which continued through most of the long night.

The next day was clear and cold but the mud was still a serious problem. By nightfall the order of march was reversed, the staff having passed the floundering baggage wagons during the day. The result was that the officers and their escort had the shelter of Fort Dodge that night while the baggage train still slithered around in the mud some miles to the north.

Andrews promptly found an acquaintance. A sutler at the post proved to be a former cow hand and he provided good sleeping accommodations for the two scouts. Still the night was not wholly comfortable. An alarm shortly after midnight turned out the garrison. Neither Andrews nor Malloy left their quarters but they could hear a considerable amount of gunfire and in the morning they learned that a sentry had been killed by the raiders.

'I hope this isn't a sample of army brains for this part of the country,' Malloy said grimly when he looked over the fort in daylight. 'It's just about everything that a fort shouldn't be. Easy approaches for an enemy, low ground—everything wrong.'

'Probably be worse as we go along,' Andrews commented cheerfully.

The baggage train dragged in about ten o'clock and the column was reorganized for the march down the valley of the Arkansas. They were in hostile country now and straggling would carry its own penalty. Shortly after noon the advance began again, this time with a detachment of Osage Indian scouts taking the lead. Pepoon's company followed them closely while Lebo's troop of cavalry formed the rear guard. Malloy and Andrews rode with Lebo's men.

They worked down the north bank of the river to the crossing, which proved a serious matter. Quicksand and ice posed a troublesome problem and the two irregulars found a quick market for their experienced services. Both men had known the difficulties of taking cattle across swollen streams and they went to work with the laboring wagoners. By the time the crossing was effected darkness was coming down again so the column went into camp just beyond the river.

Another day of backbreaking work saw them through the sandhill region and at Bluff Creek they met two companies of the Nineteenth Kansas. For the first time Malloy and Andrews found themselves a regular part of the command but it seemed to make little difference. The militia major in command of the volunteers had no orders concerning them, nor did he seem interested. They went into camp with the Kansans but they were still pretty much on their own.

The following day saw some improvement in the organization of the force. Now numbering some three hundred enlisted men with all the officers, orderlies, drivers and other camp followers it was a command about which Indians would think twice before attacking. Still the column moved with videttes and flankers out at all times. Now Malloy found himself occupied, covering the advance with Andrews on the extreme right.

After a night's camp on the Cimarron they pushed forward in similar fashion to spend the next night on an island in Beaver River. The position was not as strong as it seemed and there were two attacks during the night by raiding parties which crept in along the dry beds of the divided stream.

At three in the morning the entire command was roused and put on the alert, anticipating that a heavy attack might come at dawn. Nothing happened, however, and at daylight the march was resumed. Malloy and Andrews went out with the advance guard, not learning until evening that the Kansas Volunteers had remained behind to establish a post for protection of later baggage trains. As a result they found themselves in the same strange position as when they had left Fort Hays.

'I sure can get myself into funny messes,' Malloy said ruefully. 'Back in Hays I was in more kinds of trouble than I could count—and didn't know what any of it was really about. A month ago I was sure of just one thing: I didn't want any part of the army. So here I am.'

'Yo' don't sound so sour,' Willie observed. 'I'd almost figure yo' kinda liked it.'

Malloy smiled. 'I don't feel as disgusted as I should. This outfit is shaking down into a pretty good-looking crowd. The march has made soldiers of some of them. Whether they'll be Indian fighters is another matter.'

His approval did not last long. On the following day they approached Camp Supply and a blue column could be seen coming out to meet them. From his position on the flank Malloy did not realize the nature of the oncoming troop until the cold air resounded to the rollicking notes of *Garry Owen.*

'I take it all back,' he said to himself. 'The army is still just a parade outfit. Right in the middle of an Indian campaign Custer sends his band out to serenade Sheridan! I give upl'

Willie rode up behind him just in time to hear the final comment. 'Don't [illegible],' he [illegible]. 'A little music never hurt nobody. Say! That's a right nice tune. I oughta learn that one.'

'You ought to learn some tune,' Malloy retorted. 'I've listened to a dozen of your ditties and there wasn't a real tune to be found in any of 'em.'

Andrews did not bother to reply. He was already humming the air to himself, evidently improvising a set of words for future use.

A quick look at Camp Supply helped to reduce Malloy's sense of disappointment. Custer might parade his band under ridiculous circumstances but he had his men in good fighting trim. The camp was well designed, equipment was in excellent order and the men were in fine spirits despite the weather. Andrews and Malloy were assigned to quarters with the civilian scouts of the Seventh Cavalry and from these sturdy gentlemen they learned a number of facts which they could not have picked up by mere observation.

As usual, Andrews found an acquaintance, a lanky, drawling individual named Jack Corbin. He was bearded and dirty but he spoke unusually good English and seemed to be in the confidence of General Custer, a fact which did not keep him from gossiping.

'More damned politics being played around here,' he told them at supper. 'Sully's mad because Custer went over his head to lick this outfit into shape. I reckon it was kind of a slap the way Custer did it, particularly when they already had a battle on over who ranked who. So today Custer goes out with his band to meet General Sheridan and get in a first word before Sully can speak his piece. I guess you know who wins the argument now.'

'Always politics,' Malloy said shortly. 'You can't fight Indians that way.'

Corbin chuckled. 'I'm for Custer,' he announced. 'I don't know as I'm keen on the fancy didoes he cuts up but he sure made an army out of this mob!'

'So he's a good organizer. Can he fight?'

Corbin winked slyly. 'We'll soon know. The Cheyennes made seven kinds of a jackass out of Custer last summer and he's spoiling to get even with 'em. Maybe he does some fool things in camp but when it comes to a knock-down fight he's Johnny-on-the-spot. Last year he couldn't get the red brethren to stay and fight. In a winter campaign it'll be different; he'll be able to use his bull-headed tactics.'

Malloy did not argue. Having seen the strength of the force at Camp Supply he was inclined to agree with Corbin. Deprived of their freedom of movement, the Indians would have a hard time matching Custer's power. In addition to eleven troops of the Seventh there were in camp five companies of regular infantry and the assorted troops brought by Sheridan. That meant at least a thousand effectives not counting Osage or civilian scouts. Maybe this time there would be a campaign that would put an end to Indian [illegible] on the plains.

On the following morning Malloy had an encounter which left him puzzled. Snow had started to fall shortly after dawn and the regular picket was promptly reinforced by troops and scouts. Malloy, riding out toward the picket line with Jack Corbin, came face to face with Walter Loeffler.

Malloy stiffened, expecting some sort of trouble with the man who had stirred up such a hornet's nest in Hays City. The burly lieutenant scowled angrily, then seemed to smother his ire to speak with a sarcastic good humor. 'So you couldn't stay away from it, eh, Sid?' he remarked, the words carrying a thinly veiled sneer.

'I'm not here for the fun of it,' Malloy replied, a little puzzled at Loeffler's self-control. He had expected an explosion but his old enemy seemed to have taken a leaf from Carlton Brone's book, He was playing the good-natured act, even though it wasn't much of a job.

'What's your company?' Loeffler asked.

'Nineteenth Kansas. Civilian scout.'

'Humph! Glad they've finally got somebody in camp. The whole regiment was supposed to be here by this time.'

He turned away abruptly, leaving Malloy and Corbin to ride on into the thickening snow. Corbin broke the tight silence with a question. 'Know that man pretty well, do you?'

'Too well.'

'Right. I just thought you ought to know his reputation in camp. The men figure he ain't to be trusted.'

'Smart men. I found it out the hard way.'

The snowfall lasted all day, blanketing the camp and reducing daily drills to a minimum. Consequently it came as something of a surprise when orders were read at sundown and the men knew that they were to march at dawn. Separate instructions came to the scouts and for the first time there were orders for Malloy and Andrews. They were to ride with the scouts of the Seventh.

In the shack there was much wagging of heads, most of the scouts bewailing a fate which would take them out into the blizzard.

'Only way to ketch Injuns,' a burly, red-bearded man insisted. 'Jest last week I tole the gen'ril . . .

'When you were chief scout?' Corbin interrupted.

The remark brought a roar of laughter and Corbin explained solemnly to Andrews, 'This disreputable old he-bear is generally called California Joe. He ain't as useless as he looks, being almost smart in some ways. When Custer first hit camp he looked around for the ugliest man he could find, figuring no scout was worth his salt unless he had a face that could scare a Kiowa squaw. Joe was it. So he made California Joe Chief of Scouts. Tell 'em what happened, Joe.'

The red-bearded man grinned broadly, evidently not at all disturbed by the raillery. 'I celebrated a mite,' he drawled. 'Seems as how I got lickered up more'n usual and next thing I knowed I was takin' some o' the boys out to show 'em how scoutin' oughter be did.'

'The rest he only knows from hearsay,' Corbin chuckled. 'I was with him but I wasn't quite so lit as Joe. We got into the picket line and Joe yelled that Injuns was attackin' the camp. The pickets must have believed him because right away everybody was shooting, us shooting at the pickets and them shooting at us. Lucky we was too drunk to aim and pickets can't shoot nohow. Wasn't a soul hurt.'

'So I ain't Chief Scout no more,' Joe summarized sadly. 'But me and the gen'ril understand each other. Soon as I tole him about some o' the Injun sign I been a-seein' he made up his mind to start movin'. So here we go.'

They had a drink on that and scattered to their various makeshift quarters. With the prospect of a hard ride into a howling storm on the morrow they would need a full night of rest. For Malloy that rest did not come easily. There were too many tangled thoughts in which the trim figure of Helen Temple moved pleasantly through the shadow cast by Walter Loeffler, Carlton Brone and a fat man who refused to stay dead.

11

The clamor of trumpets routed out the camp before Malloy had stopped shivering in his cold blankets. Four o'clock on a bitter, stormy morning in late November was scarcely the hour for martial enthusiasm and thc mcn rolled out with a reluctance that quickly showed itself in their work. There was a maximum of confusion and profanity, a minimum of energy used in packing and preparation. Troopers and scouts saddled shivering horses while teamsters worked in the knee-deep snow to get the baggage wagons ready. Everywhere sullen men grumbled at the orders which sent them out on such a morning.

At dawn it was still snowing hard, a wet sticky snow which plastered itself upon men and equipment to invest the whole camp with a spectral aspect. The furtive, half light of the reluctant day only seemed to add an additional chill as numbed men climbed into wet saddles and awaited the command to form ranks.

Malloy strapped up his own outfit without delay and, accompanied by Andrews, made his way to scout headquarters. Men were grumbling there also but California Joe seemed entirely happy about the decision to move. 'Sheridan wants to hold up a spell,' he told the officers with a grin of satisfaction, 'but Custer ain't the feller to let snow stop any campaign he's hankerin' to fight. We're goin' out even if it turns into a sure enough ring-tailed blizzard.'

Still there was no order for the advance and word went around that Custer and Sheridan were still arguing. Malloy was beginning to hope that the march would be delayed but the hopes were quickly blasted. The marching orders came, typical Custer orders. Even with a foot of snow on the ground the Seventh would break camp in style. The shivering band lined up in front of headquarters, thawing their instruments as best they could while the final instructions were shouted down the lines. Then, tooting grimly away at something which sounded like *The Girl I Left Behind Me*, they played the head of the column out into the driving snow.

Custer and his staff led the way into the swirl of gray storm, the scouts following them until the formalities of departure were over. Then the commander snapped an order to his staff and the officers pulled aside to let the scouts take the lead. That would be the order of march. The white scouts broke trail, followed by the staff and then by the Osages under Hard Robe and Little Beaver. Behind the Indians the long blue column swung into action, the rear brought up by the wagon train and a rear guard of half a company.

Even as the snow stung his face and forced him to ride with his eyes almost shut Malloy was conscious of the irony of his position. From the first he had disclaimed any desire to involve himself in army matters—yet here he was, at the head of the column, helping scout for some eleven hundred men, most of them regulars of the Seventh United States Cavalry. Seven hundred drill field soldiers and a complete baggage train were going out into a blizzard which would have made experienced hunters and trappers hesitate. It would have been absurd if it had not been so serious.

The determined efforts of the regimental band faded in the distance, to be replaced by the sounds of the storm and the creak of equipment. Camp was well behind; now the problem was the difficult one of finding a trail in a world of driving snow. Visibility was so poor that only the nearer objects could be discerned and these were so shrouded in sticky snow that nothing could be recognized. There simply was no trail.

Malloy reckoned that they had slogged

forward less than two miles when California Joe and Jack Corbin halted to confer in low tones. Their gestures were eloquent. They had committed the unpardonable sin of the scout; they were already lost.

Neither was too proud to admit it. They called the other scouts around them and presently Custer and his staff came up. Joe stated the case flatly and the general asked a couple of sharp questions. No one was sure of anything. Then Hard Robe and the Osages came into the council. They, too, had lost their bearings. Malloy suspected that the column had started to circle and Corbin's words indicated that he was thinking the same thing.

'We'd better back-trail along the column,' he suggested. 'Get a line on how we're headed. We'd look awful dumb bustin' into camp again.'

'We go on,' Custer decided brusquely. From the depths of his buffalo coat he produced a small compass and ordered the scouts to follow. There was some muttering but the commander was already bucking the storm. Something in his manner brought a little confidence and his subordinates trailed along behind him.

Malloy lost track of time after that. All he knew was that he had been in the saddle for cold, weary hours, knowing nothing of direction or surroundings. All that seemed to matter was that fur-clad figure out there ahead with the little compass in his mittened hand. Then, suddenly it was late afternoon and there was a flurry of talk among the scouts. California Joe had spotted a familiar grove of trees.

'By gosh, the gen'ril's done it!' he shouted. 'This here's right close to Wolf Crick. It'll make a good camp.'

Other scouts agreed. General Custer had used his compass and his famous luck to bring them fifteen miles through the blizzard to a camping spot. Maybe the man had peculiar ideas on the subject of parades and bands but he had succeeded where Indians and trained scouts had failed.

It was a dreary camp, eighteen inches of snow on the ground and no sign of abatement in the storm. Still the column had made progress. That helped to ease some of the aches and discomforts of half-frozen men.

On the following day the weather turned clear but the march was just as difficult, no greater distance being covered than on the first day. The heavy snow impeded both troops and wagons as they plowed forward along the banks of Wolf Creek, the scouts searching constantly for Indian sign. It was not likely that many tribesmen would be out so soon after the storm but the searchers kept a vigilant watch, relieving each other at short intervals to minimize the risk of snow blindness. Malloy took several short tricks at the head of the column during the day, seeing nothing important and riding at other times with his eyes almost shut.

The next day was much the same except that California Joe called for a change in direction. It was time to leave Wolf Creek and cross a little divide into the valley of the Canadian. No one argued with him. General Custer had lost his earlier confidence in his own ability to find a trail and he issued orders only on advice of his scouts. Malloy did not know anything about this country and could work up little interest anyway. After three days of shivering in the saddle he was completely disgusted that he had not remained in Hays City to attack the disturbing problems there.

The little army camped that night on a branch of the Canadian, the men weary and restless from the long hours and the cold. There was much grumbling in camp, particularly when someone mentioned that the morrow would be Thanksgiving Day.

'Precious little reason to be thankful,' Corbin growled. 'The bluebellies are mighty down. If we don't get action soon we'll be having desertions.'

'Where would they desert to?' Malloy asked with a wry smile. 'Nothing around us but snow.'

'Soldiers won't think about that,' Corbin replied. 'They're tired enough to try anything.'

Thanksgiving Day was at least different,

even though it brought nothing for which to be thankful. The ice-filled Canadian had to be crossed. California Joe, more than half drunk, went into a long conference with the Osages, talking volubly as though to offset the fact that he could speak their tongue no better than they spoke his. Fox, the interpreter, tried to help but he was waved aside peremptorily and Joe announced that there were two fords available. One, which he knew about, was less than a mile below. The other, according to the Osages, was some four miles up-stream. Either was passable for wagons.

Custer was dubious. Joe's sources of information did not seem too reliable, considering his condition and lack of understanding between him and the Osages. There was a conference between the officers of the staff and then orders were given for a division of the column. General Custer was to lead the main body downstream and try to find Joe's ford while Major Elliot was to take Troops G, H, and M in a hunt for the crossing recommended by the Osages. Corbin, Malloy and three Indians were assigned to Elliot's command.

It meant an added unpleasantness for Malloy; he found himself riding almost stirrup to stirrup with Walter Loeffler, whose G Troop led the march. The lieutenant said nothing to him, however, and the detachment rode out into the morning sun with the three

Osages in the lead. The snow was melting now and the travel was not quite so difficult. Still the raw dampness of the morning was almost as bad as the sterner cold of the previous days. [illegible] seemed raw.

[illegible] storm, leaving a plain trail behind them. They had been headed south, without baggage.

That meant a war party and Major Elliot issued quick orders. Corbin was to ride back and inform Custer of the discovery. The three troops of cavalry were to follow the trail until different orders could come from the commander. It seemed clear from Elliot's excited tone that he had high hopes of overtaking the Indians before Custer could arrive to take a share of the glory.

The troop horses splashed through the shallows as Corbin disappeared on the back trail. Their riders were alert now. The cold, dreary hours of tiresome riding were behind them. It was still cold but now there was a prospect of action ahead. Men tested their Spencer repeaters and worked the mittens loose on stiff right hands. They were riding a new kind of trail now.

In spite of himself Malloy found his pulses quickening. He knew that there was no reason for him to get excited. These Indians were not necessarily hostiles. The column was now in territory where Indians were permitted by the terms of the treaty. It would be something of a let-down now to come across a friendly village.

With the thought he realized that there would be no such discovery. Custer and Elliot were out after Indians. They would not be too careful about looking first and attacking afterward.

He rode with Hard Robe, the troops following at a brisk pace as the trail bore off to the south again. Even in the melted snow it was possible to guess the age of the trail and it quickly became apparent that there would be no immediate clash. These Indians had passed along here soon after the snow had ceased falling.

Malloy reported the fact to Major Elliot and a reduction of speed was ordered. They went on at the steady walk which Sheridan's tactics prescribed. There was no reason to founder horses when there might be days of hard travel yet ahead. In mid-afternoon there were shouts from the rear and Elliot pulled up to wait. It was Corbin returning on a fresh horse.

The column halted for a brief rest while he reported. Already the balance of the regiment was on its way to join the hunt, only a few sick or poorly mounted troopers remaining behind to guard the baggage train. The order was for Elliot to push on until dark, then to wait for the rest of the command. This might be the great opportunity to strike a telling blow and it was not to be bungled by having a small force blunder upon the Indians in the darkness.

The first flush of ardor died away as the [illegible]

Darkness came down with the temperature and the column plunged ahead into the gloom, only the crackling roar of crusted snow being crushed beneath many hoofs serving to remind each man that he was not alone in the night. At eight o'clock Major Elliot reluctantly called a halt. They camped where the steep banks of a little creek offered shelter from the biting wind and screened the light of the fires from any hostile eyes. Coffee was soon bubbling in the mess tins and hard rations were broken out to go with it. Tired men, warmed by a bit of food and hot coffee, threw themselves down in the snow to snatch whatever rest might be obtained before the arrival of those other troopers coming up behind them.

Malloy lost himself in sleep almost as soon as he had rolled himself in his blankets. His eyes burned painfully after so much steady gazing into the brilliance of sunlit snow and in the simple relief of closing them he lost consciousness. As on the eve of the march it seemed like scant seconds before he was awakened. This time, however, there was no trumpet to arouse him, only the crunch of cavalry horses breaking the crusted snow of the back trail. The main body under General Custer was arriving.

Troopers stirred the fires, providing water for the renewed coffee making which the newcomers would demand. Major Elliot and the troop captains gathered to meet General Custer. Within a matter of minutes the little camp was full of men, the weary new arrivals hurrying to the fires and repeating the acts which Elliot's men had so recently performed. In their case, however, there was no opportunity for rest after the hasty meal. General Custer was excited and loud, showing no trace of weariness as he paced to and fro, listening almost grudgingly to the comments of Elliot, Corbin and California Joe. His every move indicated his impatience to be on the trail again, weariness forgotten in the excitement of the moment. Custer, the headlong attack specialist, was scenting battle. Somewhere ahead were Indians, a hundred warriors who had made a trail and other Indians with whom they would join forces. No one knew that they were hostiles or that their numbers were not overwhelming—but Custer certainly did not care.

In spite of his misgivings Malloy found himself admiring the man. It took energy to prosecute an Indian campaign and Custer had it. The commander had planned to strike winter-bound Indians and he was not going to be swerved from that purpose. Malloy could only hope that the general's tactical ability [illegible] brisk order passed along by non-coms. Custer at least knew when to drop the noisier formalities.

Malloy went forward with the advance guard. A last-quarter moon was rising above the trees to provide an eerie light for the march and the trail stood out plainly in its rays. The column crossed several patches of woodland where gaunt trees cast ghostly shadows in the moonlight, then Little Beaver signed for a halt, muttering gutturals to the interpreter.

'He says we're gettin' close to a village,' Fox reported to the scouts. 'Better hold up 'til the general gets here.'

Custer was right on their heels and when he heard the report he snapped his orders without hesitation. Little Beaver and Hard Robe were to walk on ahead. Mounted men were to remain a discreet distance behind them, carefully avoiding any noises which might betray the column. The shadowy line of tense, shivering troopers would lag even more. Nothing must be done to alarm the savages ahead. This time the Indians would have to stand and fight.

Malloy remained with the scouts immediately behind the Osages. With battle so close at hand he was a little surprised at the way his thoughts kept turning to distant matters. He found himself regarding the approaching conflict in a curiously detached fashion, almost as though he were a mere spectator and not a part of the attacking force. He was impressed in spite of his prejudices against formal armies. It had taken discipline and organization to bring tired, half-frozen men through the night and have them ready to fight now. Irregulars would never have made the advance so promptly; certainly they would not now be ready for an assault. Custer's men were ready, however.

The thought was subconscious. For the most part his mind dwelt on puzzles he had left behind him. Would he ever find the opportunity to improve his relations with Helen Temple? Would the Carey mix-up continue to haunt him? What had happened to Thatcher Vance? What was Brone's game and how did it fit into the other angles of the Hays City picture?

Then he looked behind him at the dim line of dark forms coming across the snow and he brought himself back to the present. He was in the midst of something big, something too important to be shrugged off with casual appreciative thoughts about efficiency and order. Seven hundred men were coming up to kill Indians. Of the seven hundred not many [illegible] risk death for such a vague cause. Maybe that had been his quarrel with the army all along; it made machines out of men. It was efficient in its own peculiar way—but was it necessarily good to have that sort of efficiency?

He shook his head angrily. The last moments before a battle were not the time for such philosophy. Right or wrong, he was here for a purpose, a deadly one. Under such circumstances a man owed it to himself to keep his mind on the grim business of staying alive.

As though to help him concentrate on the matter at hand his nostrils caught a brief tang of wood smoke. Not much of a whiff, just a hint of smoke that was whisked away quickly by the light breeze.

He knew that they had been working downgrade for some time, apparently into the valley of the Washita. Smoke here might indicate either the presence of hostile Indians or of a camp of friendly tribesmen who had been ordered here under the protection of General Hazen at Fort Cobb. No one else seemed to pay any attention to that latter possibility so Malloy decided to ignore it also. It wasn't his business to remind the commander that they might be on the verge of attacking friends. Still it was not a happy thought with those Osage scouts creeping to the top of the low ridge ahead. Their stealthy actions were an almost certain indication that a village was just beyond.

12

The scouts cut their pace at sight of the Osages' tactics. Behind them the line of troopers slowed also to maintain the interval. Even the horses appeared to sense the developing climax. They did not seem to be crunching the crusted snow quite so noisily now. Presently there was a complete halt on the part of the Indians and then Little Beaver ran back to announce that they had found the remains of a small campfire.

He was promptly surrounded by scouts and staff officers. 'Pony herders' fire,' California Joe suggested as Custer approached. 'That means the village ain't fur off.'

General Custer issued new orders quickly and crisply. He was visibly elated now, thumping his saddle horn with big mittened fists. 'Keep right on as we're going,' he ordered. 'Pass the word back for extra care. Don't let the horses make a sound.'

They waited until Little Beaver had joined [illegible] hoofs in what seemed like a veritable roar. It was almost painful to hear it, yet Malloy told himself that it could not have been heard a hundred yards.

The gradual down slope seemed to be composed of a series of terraces and they could see the Osages flatten out as they reached the edge of the next drop. Custer interpreted the move without hesitation. 'Halt right here,' he commanded brusquely, sliding from the saddle even as he spoke. Then he ran forward to join the Indians.

The silence of the dying night was almost stifling as the scouts waited for his return. From the rear there was only a faint creak of leather and a muffled stamping of hoofs. Out in front there was no sound at all, only those dark figures huddled together in the moonlight. It was in the midst of this tense hush that they heard the sound which was significant yet disquieting. From somewhere down there in the valley came the faint cry of a child. An Indian baby had wailed.

Even as the men stiffened they caught another sound. A bell had tinkled briefly on the frosty air.

'We're close,' Corbin whispered hoarsely. 'There's the pony herd.'

No one commented on the child's cry. It was not pleasant to think of what would soon happen down there along the Washita. There would be no time to distinguish between warriors and non-combatants when the attack started.

Custer came back at a run. 'The Osages were worried,' he said with a grim smile. 'They didn't know whether they were looking at a herd of buffalo or a mob of warriors in ambush. It's really a pony herd. That means a sizeable village.' He swung into the saddle and snapped an order.

'My compliments to troop and battalion commanders. Have them halt the men where they are and leave them to prepare for the attack. Officers above platoon commanders to meet me here as quickly as possible.'

With that he seemed to shed some of the tension, chatting easily with the scouts about the probable size of the village which was down there among the trees. The Osages came back then, showing signs of worry. Fox listened to them for some minutes, then interpreted their words to the commander. 'They're afraid the village is too big for us to handle,' he reported. 'They think we ought to wait until daylight.'

'Children!' Custer scoffed. 'This is the Seventh Cavalry, man! Tell them that. Tell [illegible] can whip any Indian [illegible] such rashness [illegible] He might be sending men to their deaths by such a blind attack.

'Some day he'll git too cocky,' Willie Andrews whispered. 'It's all right to think yo're good—but there's a hell of a lot of Injuns.'

Malloy grunted noncommittally and sat back to watch the general's council-of-war. Doubt was heavy in his mind once more. It was heartening to watch the orderly lines of troopers moving into their appointed positions but it was not encouraging to know that they were being sent blindly against an unknown enemy. Military efficiency had its good points, no doubt, but it could not overcome the one fatal defect. It was in the long run dependent upon intelligent command.

He watched preparations with mingled feelings but it was only when the first streaks of red dawn crept up out of the eastern ridges that he saw a sight which brought all of his disgust back. The regimental band was forming just back of the last concealing ridge, its members working industriously to thaw their frozen instruments. Of all places in the world to bring a military band! This was even more ridiculous than the welcoming reception to Sheridan. There was something callous, even cruel in sending men into action against an unscouted foe to the tune of—probably *Garry Owen.*

He watched with an angry fascination while the musicians struggled with frozen keys and worked over mouth-pieces which might freeze fast to chapped lips. It was almost unbelievable that in this winter-bound wilderness troops were actually to be played into battle. Over all that frozen trail men had struggled forward for no purpose but to blow horns! The asininity of it was not funny. Even on a grim job like this one the professional soldier had to have his spit and polish.

Corbin interrupted his ruminations. 'Malloy, you ride with Major Elliot. You'll swing wide to the left and come in from the other side of the village. Don't cut it too close; we don't want to give the show away until everybody's in position. The major will leave it up to you to pick the trail. When you're ready to go in he'll take command. The band will give the signal to charge but you don't need to pay any attention. Your job ain't fightin'; that's for troopers.'

His brief grin at mention of the band

indicated that he was of the same mind with Malloy. That part of the attack plan was beyond the comprehension of a man who knew plains Indians and the best methods of fighting them.

[illegible] sides and trapping them against the ice-filled Washita. Malloy quickly joined Elliot's G, H, and M troops, his mind a little bitter with thoughts of the band—and of the Indian child he had heard crying down there in the predawn blackness. The two did not seem to go well together.

Then he forced his attention to the duty at hand. He had to pick a path for Elliot's men to reach the lower valley without betraying their presence. That was his job; he was supposed to be able to spot the proper course even though he had never seen the country before.

Using the little patches of cover to the best possible advantage he led the way in a wide circle, presently striking the Washita at a spot which he believed to be only a couple of hundred yards from the village. Elliot promptly disposed his men in line of attack, the three companies fanning out behind Malloy as he moved cautiously toward the Indian town. Almost immediately he could see their objective through the trees and he signed for a halt, the men poised for the order to charge.

Major Elliot ignored him after that, apparently having no further interest in a civilian scout of doubtful status. Malloy understood but remained close to the commander. The formalities of military procedure were bothering him again. He wasn't supposed to participate in the battle but he had every intention of doing so. A fight was a fight. The best way to get it over was to win as quickly as possible. That meant every fighting man doing a share. This was not the time to interpret rules and regulations.

He saw that Walter Loeffler was flexing his stubby fingers nervously, either limbering the cold digits or merely working off tension. Even as he noted the gesture the dawn was brutally shattered by the strident discords of half frozen musicians trying to coax music out of completely frozen horns.

Instantly Major Elliot waved his sabre in the signal for the charge but Malloy's mind refused to accept the deadly seriousness of it all. He was grinning idiotically as he plunged ahead with the troopers. That tune drifting down the frozen slope was certainly *Garry Owen,* just as he had expected. Even stiff fingers and frozen valves could not disguise its rollicking lilt. Now it did not bother him that the rowdy tune was being used as a signal for mass murder; for some ridiculous reason his thoughts turned in another direction. He was wondering what sort of verses Willie Andrews had managed to concoct for it.

It was a fleeting humor. He was in the van [illegible] saw that the village was not a large one, probably containing some two hundred warriors. He also saw that they were Cheyennes and the sight made him feel better. Cheyennes were legitimate enemies. The blind attack was not going to turn into a colossal blunder after all.

The clatter of the repeating Spencer carbines enveloped the village as the soldiers closed in, the scattering fire of the Cheyennes sounding puny by comparison. Malloy swept forward, picking his targets deliberately so as to avoid the killing of women or children, and found himself exchanging shots with a pair of almost naked savages. He fired at one of the warriors just as the Indian discharged his own rifle and in the split second of desperate action he was conscious of two facts. The Indian was crumpling but his hasty shot had taken effect. Malloy's horse was going down.

He threw himself sideways as he fell, rolling to dodge the dying struggles of the horse and at the same time recover himself to defend against that other warrior. He came to his knees with the six-gun ready for action but there was no enemy left. A trooper had cut him down.

Strangely enough, that seemed to be the situation on all sides. The battle had ended as suddenly as it had begun. The charging troopers, firing their repeaters as they came in to close quarters, had mowed down the Indians ruthlessly, simply blanketing the village with lead. The battle had been a massacre.

At only one point was there any real action still going on. The Cheyennes were making good a retreat where Elliot's right flank had not quite made a junction with Thompson's B company. It left an avenue of escape downstream and through this a handful of Indians were fleeing in disorder.

Malloy ran to report the fact but Major Elliot had already seen it. He shouted a command to the nearest troopers and dashed away, gathering followers as he rode. By that time the attacking force had become thoroughly tangled and the men who followed Elliot were from several different troops. Malloy started toward a riderless horse but was diverted as a white woman ran from a nearby tepee. He turned aside to help her but before he could take more than a couple of strides a second figure appeared at the door of the lodge. A fat Indian squaw, moving with savage speed despite her bulk, lunged forward to seize the white woman and drive a long knife into her abdomen. Just as quickly the squaw was shot by a trooper.

[illegible] sort of wanton savagery he had just witnessed.

He bent over the unfortunate woman but saw at once that there was nothing to be done. The knife stroke had been a vicious slash rather than a stab, making a wound which was too huge for any quick treatment. The woman died in his arms and he stood up again, his feeling toward General Custer a completely different one. Maybe extermination was the proper slogan for an Indian war after all. Certainly there could be no compromise with such brutal instincts as that.

He looked around him briefly, wondering what his next move should be. At a little distance he could hear Custer shouting orders for consolidating the quick victory. Indians were beginning to gather in some force on the bluffs below the captured village and it seemed probable that they represented other nearby tribes. Already there had been a weak attack made on the troopers who had been left behind to guard equipment. The Seventh could not yet rest upon its laurels.

A troop was sent back to pick up the extra equipment which had been laid aside by men lightening themselves for the attack while a couple of squadrons deployed to open long-range fire upon those Indians on the bluffs. Suddenly Malloy recalled Major Elliot's hasty departure. The officer with his handful of men had gone directly into the area where the Indian strength seemed greatest.

A riderless horse stood trembling near one of the village huts so Malloy took possession of the animal and rode across to the nearest officer. He explained about Major Elliot and was sent on to Custer. The commander knew nothing of Elliot's move either. In the flurry of battle no one had witnessed the hurried action. Oddly enough, no one seemed to be interested now. Custer merely accepted the information and went on with what he was doing.

A little puzzled, Malloy crossed to where Corbin and California Joe were standing. At a time like this it seemed probable that scouts would be used to get a line on the absent men. He talked it over with Corbin but received only a dour grin. 'The general ain't bothering himself with us now,' Corbin growled. 'Our job's just tracking. Sit tight; he'll get over his excitement pretty soon.'

Malloy watched impatiently while Lieutenant Godfrey was sent out with a part of K troop to round up the Indian pony herd.

After that he thought a detachment would be sent on Elliot's trail but Custer seemed interested only in the conquered village. He interfered but slightly with the Osages who were plundering the place, putting all his [illegible] The lieutenant rode directly to General Custer and reported something which Malloy did not overhear. There was a brief exchange of words but the report did not divert Custer from the work of destruction. Godfrey shrugged a little, then set his men to the same task.

The Indians on the downstream bluffs were keeping up a scattering fire now so two full troops were sent against them, making a charge that was just long enough to drive the snipers away. Walter Loeffler had been one of the officers in charge of the sally and when the brief skirmish was over he went promptly to General Custer. Malloy could see him talking earnestly, as Godfrey had done, but he did not seem to bc getting anywhere. Custer almost ignored him.

Loeffler went back to speak briefly with a pair of brother officers, then he turned and came directly toward the little group of civilian scouts.

'Malloy,' he said abruptly, 'they tell me you

saw Major Elliot ride out of the village. That right?'

'Yes.'

'Well, we're afraid he's trapped there along the creek—but the general won't do anything about it.' The last seemed to come out with difficulty. 'Lieutenant Godfrey heard firing down that way when he was rounding up the Indian ponies. My men heard it too. If we could get a scout's report maybe we could get the general to order a relief expedition out.'

'Won't he believe you?' Malloy asked bluntly.

Loeffler did not show the indignation which might have been expected. He was too worried. 'I don't know why he won't but he won't. And if Major Elliot's in a trap we've got to get help to him. We'd never be able to face it if we left him out there without aid.'

So that was it, Malloy thought. Major Elliot had to be rescued—because it would be hard on somebody's reputation otherwise. Still the same old business of playing the game according to the rules.

'We can't do anything for you,' Corbin said shortly. 'Our orders are to stay here until the general passes on his next instructions. We can't go scouting on our own.'

'Malloy can,' Loeffler retorted. 'He's not working for the Seventh Cavalry.'

Malloy nodded quickly, forcing himself to ignore the little warnings which popped into his mind. 'I'll go. I know what direction he went.'

'I'll go part way with you,' Loeffler said. 'Maybe I can pick up some sort of partial report to bring in while you're picking up the [illegible] partial report. That was something out of the past, something better forgotten just now. Walter Loeffler's anxiety was real, regardless of its source. The job was to find Elliot and those troopers who had gone with him.

13

They struck boldly into the timber along the river. It was better to take the chance of meeting Indians there than it was to advertise their move by riding across the more open bottom lands. This way they were at least hidden from the savages on the bluffs. Malloy picked up the trail as soon as they reached the river bank, the snow telling a plain story. Nineteen cavalry horses had galloped downstream, hard on the trail of an indeterminate number of mounted and running Indians.

'That must be Major Elliot,' Loeffler grunted. 'A hasty count showed eighteen men missing. They're with him.'

'With him—but where?' Malloy muttered.

It was ominously silent down there among the snow-covered trees. As they approached a bend of the Washita they could hear an occasional shot from behind them as troopers dug out skulking Indians, but ahead there was only silence, a silence which under the circumstances was men-acing. There could be no doubt that somewhere ahead was a large number of Indians and a small detachment of soldiers. Why was there no shooting? It was not pleasant to consider the probable answer.

They rounded the river bend and the distant roll of small arms brought them to an abrupt halt. Malloy felt a momentary sense of relief but realized his mistake even before Loeffler could gesture toward the rear and say, 'That's our men killing the Indian horses. General Custer figured we couldn't take them with us and he is determined to destroy everything of value to the Indians. This village will be a horrible example for all restless Indians of the future.'

'He'd be smarter to save his ammunition,' Malloy retorted. 'He might need it before he gets out of this valley. There are certain to be other villages close at hand and I don't like the way the savages are lying low. It could mean that they're getting ready to launch a big attack.'

The sound of firing became fainter as they moved on, then it took on a new note and Malloy knew that this time he was listening to [illegible] The sound was [illegible]

'He's got them!'

'Sounds like they've got him,' Malloy contradicted. 'By the noise I'd say he was pocketed.'

Loeffler pulled up abruptly, his lips tight as he spoke without looking at his companion. 'One of us ought to report back immediately while the other goes on to get a better view of the situation. I suppose you won't . . .'

'You remember, do you?' Malloy said dryly. 'I should insist on being the one to go back. Having been double-crossed once I haven't any reason to trust you this time.'

Loeffler colored but controlled himself. 'Have it your way,' he said hoarsely. 'Just so we get Elliot. There'll be hell if we don't find him.'

There it was again. No one was worrying about Elliot and his men; the only thing that mattered was the professional reputations of other officers. Custer seemed to have forgotten the point but his subordinates had not. Elliot had to be rescued in order that no one would be blamed for leaving him.

'Go on,' Malloy said disgustedly. 'I'm being a fool but it won't work that way. You're not the man to scout the Indians and I'd have no chance of beating any sense into that bull-headed general. Hurry it up. Get a relief column out here if you have to stage a mutiny to do it!'

Loeffler whirled his mount without another word, dashing away as Malloy slid from his own horse and led the animal into a thicket. From here the job would have to be done on foot. The important thing was to leave the horse in a spot where he could be found readily—but not by passing Indians.

He reconnoitered cautiously before leaving the animal, making certain that his movements had not been observed. Then he moved downstream again, on foot now and with every sense alert. Judging by the sound of firing ahead of him the Indians were fairly swarming about the beleaguered troopers, evidently trying to finish them off before help could arrive. Custer would have to move quickly if any rescue was to be effected.

He crossed a low ridge through which the river had cut its passage and as he topped the rise the sound of firing came to his ears with alarming distinctness. The fight must be in the patch of woodland just ahead and the trail under foot told a part of the story. Right here on the ridge the galloping troopers had met their first major resistance. Apparently their headlong rush had carried them a few hundred yards farther until they had been forced to dismount and take cover. Now they were [illegible]

A [illegible] adjustment of his position he could see several warriors moving about. A wounded Cheyenne staggered out of the firing line and two other Indians went forward to take his place. Other savages were working along from tree to tree, apparently keeping up a war of nerves on the trapped white men. He saw that some of the warriors carried firearms, everything from Lancaster rifles to old battered flintlocks, but others were armed with bows and arrows. That meant a close range battle. The trap was narrowing.

Intent upon the scene ahead of him Malloy neglected his own flank, awakening to his danger when a war arrow zipped into the tree just in front of his face, its gaudy shaft quivering against his left ear. He turned quickly to see an Indian fitting a second arrow to his bow.

Malloy side-stepped and brought up his Colt in the same motion. Its boom came none too soon, the Indian arrow flying wildly into the air as the archer crumpled with a howl.

Malloy did not wait to investigate further. That gunshot from the Indian rear would certainly bring warriors out of the battle line. Scouts certainly must have been covering their rear against the advance of more troopers; he had been lucky that he had not run into more trouble than he had. He sprinted for the nearest clump of bushes, covering almost fifty yards of open ground before a bullet whistled over his head. A chorus of yells came with it and he knew that the chase was on. Now it was not only Major Elliot and his eighteen men who needed help from those idle soldiers back there in the Washita village. Sid Malloy would be quite willing to swallow a lot of harsh sentiments about the regulars if he could just see a line of blue jackets coming through the woods.

He sped through the little patch of cover, crossing another open stretch before the pursuers could spot him. It was no time to make a stand; in this country he would be surrounded quickly if he tried it. His only chance of survival was to get clean away.

He looked behind him once as he plunged into the next lot of trees, just in time to see a tall Indian come loping across the crusted snow. In spite of the cold the man was almost naked and Malloy knew that in a race he would have no chance with such an antagonist. Accordingly he slowed his pace a little until the Indian was closing in rapidly, then he turned and slid behind a tree, resting his arm against the trunk to sight carefully with the .44. The Colt boomed just once, doing its grim [illegible] efficiency. Then Malloy ran on.

[illegible] spare minutes for aimless searching. They were closing in again now and he had to sprint hard to cover the next open patch ahead of them. His legs were aching and he realized that the hard ride and loss of sleep were beginning to tell on him. This race could not go on much longer.

Another backward glance told him that he had four pursuers to contend with. Too heavy odds—yet there seemed to be no other way out but to fight. Then he recognized the clump of trees where he had left his horse. It made a difficult decision. There would not be enough time for him to get the pony and make a complete getaway. If he tried it he was almost certain to have his horse shot from under him. Then the situation would be hopeless. It was better to take a chance on beating off this first attack, hoping to get a breathing spell which would permit escape.

With the thought he swung hard toward the bank of the river, taking up a position where he could not be flanked. The Indians came on at a rush, not realizing his change of strategy, and he caught them by surprise with a deadly fire. Two went down before they could check their pace, the other two taking cover.

After that it was desperate waiting, trying to keep an eye on the section of woodland where the two savages had disappeared and at the same time guarding against their almost certain attempt to flank him. The worst of it all was the fear that other Indians would come along before he could dispose of the immediate enemies. Delay was all on the side of the Cheyennes.

He held his position only a matter of seconds after getting both guns fully reloaded, then he made a quick dash for another clump of trees, hoping to draw a hasty shot which might betray the positions of his enemies. The ruse was not successful but his new position put him in a spot where he was able to see an Indian trying to approach the place where he had so recently been. Obviously the savage had not seen the white man's move, so absorbed was he in his own tactics.

Malloy fired deliberately and moved again, getting a grim joy out of his own deadly shooting. Without taking a scratch he had whittled the odds down to an even balance. Now if he could only spot that fourth Indian before more of the howling mob should arrive . . .

He waited impatiently again, the silence harder to bear than the actual danger. Nothing happened. There was no sound in the forest except the rustle of the light breeze and the distant crackle of gunfire. Perhaps the [illegible] underbrush that he understood what had happened. The remaining Indian had swung in a wide circle and had stumbled upon the hidden pony. Now he was trying to make off with the animal.

Throwing caution to the winds Malloy ran toward the sound. He was just in time to see the Cheyenne sending the bronc plunging through the woodland toward the open country downstream. The Indian was in retreat now, no longer an immediate source of danger, but his retreat might mean complete disaster. Without the horse Malloy would be trapped.

The .44 slammed viciously, swiftly, and at the fourth shot the warrior threw his head back, twisted his body and uttered a screech which only ended when his body slammed against the ground. Malloy did not wait to assure himself that his enemy was dead; he was running again as soon as the Indian started to fall, this time in pursuit of the stampeding horse.

The pony headed straight away from the river, running hard toward the lightly wooded ridges which flanked the stream. Malloy followed at a dead run, taking the risk of meeting more Indians. So far as he had been able to determine there were no warriors in that particular direction and it seemed like a good gamble to make sure of the horse. It was better than retreating up the river on foot with pursuit behind him and a chance of meeting some of the Indians who had been sniping from the bluffs.

To his relief he saw no signs of any enemy and even though he promptly lost sight of the running horse he knew by the marks in the snow that the animal was circling a little toward the captured village and not running very fast. That seemed good enough for now, even though it meant that the horse was as tired as the man.

Making a hurried estimate of the distances and directions involved in his recent movements he decided that he must be a full two miles from the main body of soldiers. Unfortunately he was now away from the river and in no position to make contact with any relief force which might be headed toward Major Elliot and his men. Still there was no sign of Indians so he speeded his pace as much as he thought he could stand, anxious to overtake the frightened pony before the animal could lead him farther into the wilderness.

He covered half a mile, his legs aching again and his breath coming with an effort. The trail was veering off to the north once more and it [illegible] trusting that some trooper might have trained the beast to recognize the signal. It worked. The horse stopped and looked around, puzzled but wary. Malloy closed in quickly, his hopes rising.

He had almost reached the runaway when his ear caught a sound of hoofbeats some distance behind and to the right. A single glance told him that he had reached the end of his brief moment of good fortune. Those riders crunching the snow there in the forest were not troopers. He broke for the waiting horse, hoping that his coaxing words would offset the alarming nature of his advance. It was now or never.

The pony waited until his deserted rider was within an arm's length, then he decided to run again. It was too late. Malloy clutched desperately at a stirrup, took a few hard knocks as the horse dragged him along, and managed to haul himself into the saddle. Only then did he look back at the riders he had seen among the trees. The sight was not cheering. Three hard-riding Cheyennes were bearing down upon him, low on their ponies' necks and with their moccasined heels drumming wildly against the animals' ribs.

Even at the distance Malloy could see that one of the enemy carried a Spencer repeater. Perhaps Elliot's men had already been wiped out or maybe this gun was spoil from some earlier skirmish around Camp Supply. One way or another it made the adverse odds all the more serious; the Indians were drawing within range and the warrior with the repeater was raising his weapon for a shot. It was a running fight after that. In a matter of about three minutes the Indians gained alarmingly on the tired cavalry mount and in the last minute of that time Malloy emptied both of his six-shooters, scoring a hit with his last shot. The slug rolled an Indian out of his makeshift saddle but it left Malloy with the problem of reloading at full gallop.

He managed to get four chambers loaded when he felt the paralyzing impact of a slug along his lower ribs. The pain and shock sickened him for a moment and he could feel himself swaying in the saddle as the agony of it went through him. Fighting the pain he turned to line his sights on the nearer Indian, triggering the Colt with fingers that already seemed numb. It was like a dream when he saw the warrior go sprawling from his horse, a ridiculous sort of a nightmare where he still aimed the gun at an empty space above a pony's back. His mind told him that there was another enemy who must be killed but his hand refused to change its aim. There was a [illegible] feet away. Even as he sighted he could feel the giddiness coming over him again. He fought the mist again, pulled the trigger and felt himself falling. He did not even feel the impact when he struck the snow but consciousness returned shortly and he knew that he was lying on the ground beside a dead Indian. After that the blackness returned and he lost all interest in everything.

14

Consciousness did not return easily to Sid Malloy. There was a long, painful period when he was vaguely aware of the cold, of cramped muscles in his legs and of stabbing pains in his side. Occasionally his head cleared for brief moments and after several of these lucid intervals he knew several facts about himself. He was lashed to the saddle of that same cavalry horse, the one which had led him such a merry chase from the river. His hands were tied to the saddle horn in front of him. Someone was riding just ahead. The moments of consciousness did not stay with him long enough for him to decide whether he was a prisoner or not. Nor did he learn the identity of the blurred figure which appeared in that annoying mist ahead of him.

Finally, however, he opened his eyes to find the mist gone. Darkness was all around him but the waning moon above the trees indicated that this time the blackness was not mental. Then he noted the glowing embers of a dying camp-fire and knew that he was seeing properly again. He remained motionless for some minutes, trying to get his bearings. He was flat on his back, covered by some sort of fur robe which tickled his chin. His hands and feet were not bound. That much he discovered almost as he remembered his wound. A cautious hand fumbled beneath the robe to discover that the injury had been crudely bandaged. The knowledge brought relief. He must be among friends.

It puzzled him a little that the hour was so late. The moon's position indicated that it was about four o'clock in the morning. He had been wounded sometime in midafternoon. A part of the ride had taken place in daylight. How long after dark had they traveled, then—and how far?

Finally he raised his head, setting his teeth as the movement brought a flood of agony to the wounded ribs. He could see that another fur-wrapped form was on the ground beside him, evidently the man who had ridden ahead [illegible]

The fact that the campfire had been built was another good sign. It must mean that they were safely out of Indian country. With that much clear in his mind he let the weariness creep over him once more and his eyes closed contentedly.

Only the merest hint of daylight was in the eastern sky when he aroused himself once more to find a squat, muffled figure bending over the fire. Just the man's broad back was visible but Malloy gained a quick impression of a short, stocky body topped by a round, shaggy head. Judging by his clothing the fellow was a trapper or a hunter.

'Hullo,' Malloy greeted, trying to make his voice sound cheerful. 'Where are we and why?' He wondered if the tones were as weak and thin as they sounded in his own ears.

The stocky man turned abruptly, displaying toothless gums in a grin that was something to see. The face matched the body. Low brows and a broad nose were about the only real features in a broad, flat face which had never been well proportioned and now sagged shapelessly around bare gums. Nose and chin seemed to meet in a whirlwind of wrinkles but there was a good-humored glint in the black eyes. Malloy felt certain that he had found a real friend even though his rescuer was one of the dirtiest individuals he had ever met.

The wrinkled lips parted to emit a sputter of sounds which Malloy decided must be Spanish. Then the face collapsed again and the eyes twinkled expectantly.

In spite of his discomfort Malloy wanted to laugh. Instead he smiled his apologies. 'Sorry, *amigo,*' he replied. *'No hablo mucho Espanol.* And, believe me, that's putting it very modestly.'

The ungainly head bobbed agreement, another spurt of words being accompanied by gestures which made it clear that Malloy was to remain where he was. It took many more gestures, along with a flood of completely useless words, to convey the rest of the message; that there were no Indians near, that the soldiers had gone away, that Malloy's wound was a bad one.

After that the squatty man went on with his breakfast preparations, giving Malloy no further attention. It was a scanty meal, the trapper apparently trying to stretch his own rations. Appreciating the man's generosity, Malloy tried to forget the dubious sanitation of the cook. It was no time to be fussy. More travel was certainly in prospect and he was going to need all the strength he could muster.

Neither man spoke again until the meal was over, then the stranger faced Malloy and [illegible]

'Malloy,' Pancho repeated carefully, repeating the name until he appeared to be satisfied with his own pronunciation of it. Then he grinned again and turned away, plunging into the brush to bring the three picketed ponies which Malloy had already noticed. One of them was the cavalry mount Malloy had been riding, the other two were mustangs which followed the trapper as though accustomed to being petted by him.

Getting the wounded man into the saddle was an arduous —and, for Malloy, a painful— job. When it was eventually accomplished Malloy was sick and dizzy, holding himself erect by force of will. Pancho studied him intently for a moment, then proceeded to lash him fast to the saddle as he had done on the previous day. Malloy was too sick to object.

He knew that they were riding away in a generally south-easterly direction but after the first few hundred yards he knew little else.

Every jolt brought back the nausea and the day's ride became a replica of the previous afternoon's experience. Spells of painful consciousness broke through the dizzy blackness but for the most part they were not long enough nor clear enough for him to know anything except pain. The wound in his side was bleeding again and a few times he rallied his thoughts enough to wonder whether he was bleeding to death. That would account for the ever-growing weakness.

He was dimly aware of climbing through wooded passes and up snow-covered slopes. He even remembered stopping at a rough log cabin nestled beneath some pines. He never recalled being lifted from the saddle and carried inside. After the sight of the cabin there was only an endless, troubled dream of blazing tepees, galloping troopers and yelling Indians. Sometimes he fought the last skirmish over again, trying to roll his body for that last final effort. It was then that he knew himself to be in the grasp of a man who would not let him turn. Sometimes the battle was a long one but always it seemed to end in the same way. He would find that the man who held him was a stocky little fellow with worried eyes and a shapeless face. Then he would relax and sleep again.

Finally he awakened to find that it was daylight once more. Pancho was not in the cabin and after a few moments' thought

Malloy moved gingerly in the crude bunk. His side was only vaguely uncomfortable now but he discovered that it took a lot of effort to move his arms and legs. The discovery brought a rueful grin. He must be all tired out from so [illegible]

[illegible] came into contact with a crop of whiskers which astonished him. To the best of his memory it had been some four days since he had last shaved. There must be a two weeks' growth of beard on his chin!

The realization that he had been out of his head for such a long time left him weaker than ever and he lay still for many minutes, trying to persuade himself that he was really conscious again and not having another crazy dream. Finally he convinced himself and at once he began to wonder about all the things he had left behind him. What had happened along the Washita? Where had the troops gone? Had Elliot been rescued? Where was Andrews? . . . For that matter, where was Malloy—and how long had he been here?

He spent most of the afternoon thinking about it, his one attempt at getting up such a marked failure that he was content to lie still and think. Just at dusk Pancho waddled into the hut and Malloy knew that his early impression had been an accurate one. The dumpy little Mexican was a trapper. The well-oiled rifle and the bundle of fresh pelts were significant marks of the trade and Malloy wondered a little guiltily how many days of trapping the squatty man had missed because of his kindness to a wounded stranger.

The beady eyes brightened at sight of Malloy's smile. '*Como está?*' Pancho asked, pronouncing the words with almost ludicrous care. During the long days of fighting his patient's fever he had evidently learned that Spanish was not one of Malloy's major accomplishments.

Malloy chuckled as the real meaning of the man's tone became apparent to him. '*Muy bueno, gracias,*' he replied, extending himself practically to the limit of his linguistic ability to add, '*Muchas gracias.*' He could only hope that the words conveyed a small part of his gratitude.

The dumpy man was delighted. He launched into another of his sputtering orations, stopping only when Malloy waved a hopeless hand.

'*No sabe,*' Malloy told him. '*No hablo mucho.*'

Pancho looked disappointed but shrugged his fat shoulders and turned away to peel out of his ragged buffalo coat. He seemed to think it a little silly that a man should know only enough of a language to state that he knew nothing of it. Malloy could appreciate the point but he was in no mood to care. Just now he did not feel energetic enough to worry about any lack of talk.

In the ensuing weeks, however, the difficulty [illegible] ideas but it was a problem to make Malloy's dozen words of Spanish and Pancho's equally slender command of English do the trick. Both understood Indian sign language, however, and gradually they began to make themselves understood. It seemed that Pancho had been headed toward the Washita villages on some errand or other and had heard the noise of the battle. He had skirted the scene cautiously, unwilling to risk himself in a situation where neither side might accept him as a friend, and had come upon Malloy just in time to witness the final brush with the mounted warriors. Why he had not made some effort to take the wounded man back to the regiment was a point which Malloy couldn't get explained.

Another point that presented difficulty was the matter of time and place. It did not seem possible that a full month had elapsed since the Washita fight but Pancho's sign language seemed definite. It was already January. Only the length of Malloy's beard made it possible for him to believe it. As to the location of the cabin the puzzle was even more complete, any signs being inadequate to convey the trapper's hazy ideas of formal geography. All Malloy could guess was that they were far to the west of the Washita settlements. The mountainous nature of the country was one clue to the location but he could not remember the maps well enough to recall what mountains might lie within the area in question.

Another month passed before his strength returned sufficiently for him to be quite himself again. By that time he had taken over all the work of the cabin and was even helping the trapper with some of the outside work. Still he was not too busy for his mind to trouble itself with the problems he had left behind him in Kansas.

There was no concern as to his immediate safety. Pancho had adequate supplies of everything on hand, even powder and lead, so that Malloy was able to make up extra cartridges for the two revolvers which the Mexican had so thoughtfully rescued. As long as the supply of caps held out there would be ammunition for the .44's and Pancho was also well armed. He felt certain that the pair of them could give a good account of themselves if the Indian war spread toward them. It was the uncertainty on other counts which brought the sense of worry.

At first he had been bitterly resentful at

Loeffler for this second abandonment but then he relented a little, realizing that his old enemy might not be to blame this time. General Custer had certainly ignored Major Elliot and his men; probably the headstrong [illegible]

[illegible] Hays City and he knew that it would be well to prepare for trouble. In all probability he had been reported as a casualty of the Washita fight, a situation which might cause a certain amount of awkwardness in establishing neglected property claims. At best there would be delay in the prosecution of his spring plans.

Most important of all was his concern over Helen Temple's actions. He had felt that some sort of vague understanding had passed between them at their last meeting but actually the girl had said or done nothing which gave him any real reason to think she would wait for him. She had not made any break with Dave Nixon, in fact her major anxiety had been on that young man's behalf. It would not be surprising if she had already married Nixon.

The very hopelessness of the situation made Malloy all the more anxious to get back to Hays City as quickly as possible. If he still had a chance with Helen he did not propose to throw it away through any unnecessary delay.

Thinking about Hays City didn't get him there. The winter dragged by with maddening deliberation, the snow holding its grip on the mountains until Malloy was about ready to believe that he had blundered into some strange region where winter was everlasting. Finally, however, the snow turned to slush and then to mud. It was time to get started, time to say farewell to the peculiar old fellow who had been such a sturdy rescuer and so pleasant, though unsanitary, a companion.

By that time the pair of them had worked out a sort of language which permitted a pretty fair exchange of ideas. English, Spanish, signs and grunts combined to serve their purpose and Pancho explained that he proposed to pack his winter's pelts to the railroad. That suited Malloy exactly and they made their preparations, packing everything except the equipment which appeared to be the regular furnishings of the cabin. Finally they rode away to the north, Pancho leading the way while Malloy rode tail, urging on the well-laden pack horses. Before many days a lot of questions would be answered and Malloy could only hope that he would like the answers. Oddly enough, he was amused to realize that the question foremost in his mind was a ridiculous one. He wanted to know whether Willie Andrews had ever contrived a set of words to go with *Garry Owen.*

15

It took a bit of riding to clear the high hill [illegible] more anxious to reach Hays City. Every day now meant added delay in the start of his summer's work as well as added risk that something might happen to the equipment he had collected during the autumn. The old regrets came back to him. If only he had remained in Hays City he might now be on his way to the Colorado country. The whole miserable winter had been caused by his own bad judgment. He should have remained to face down those crazy suspicions. Even when a man had been practically lost for four years and knew no one, he could still find ways to establish his true identity. The evidence which had been accepted in the matter of the legacy would certainly have been good enough to satisfy law officers. It had been pretty silly to let Carlton Brone talk him into running away from Thatcher Vance.

They rode rapidly but with ample caution, Pancho explaining that early war parties might be out. Malloy knew that the Washita fight might have set the whole frontier ablaze so he was entirely willing to heed the advice. He had already guessed that he had spent the winter somewhere in or near the Texas panhandle so he knew that there would be plenty of hostile Indians in the region.

For two full days after leaving the hills they came upon no trace of human life or habitation but on the third day they cut the trail of some thirty horsemen who had recently ridden toward the southeast. Both men studied the sign with due care, even following the sign for some little distance. Malloy decided that a half company of cavalry had passed the spot, either on patrol or engaged in some part of a continuing campaign. For a few minutes he was tempted to leave Pancho and ride to overtake the troopers but second thought caused him to change his mind. His real objective was Hays City; he had run into enough grief following soldiers.

Two days later he decided that they had reached western Kansas. Gone were the hills, only undulating grasslands meeting the eye as they swung a little more toward the northeast. Another full day of riding passed without incident except for occasional Indian sign but on the following day they struck a well-defined wagon trail which followed the winding course of a small river. This must be the main stage route to the west, paralleling the Smoky Hill. It did not seem possible that he was seeing signs of civilization once more but all the evidence pointed that way. The winter was over.

Pancho's signs indicated that this was [illegible] route and they began to [illegible] be greeted with any degree of cordiality. The drivers had each picked up guns while a single horseman was ranging wide from the trail, a carbine held conspicuously in front of him as he executed his flanking movement.

Malloy noted that Pancho was keeping his hands well away from any weapon, evidently anxious to convince the strangers of his peaceful intent. Malloy followed the example. Evidently the trail was still bedeviled by bandits and travelers were justly suspicious of such hard looking strangers as Malloy and the Mexican certainly were.

Suddenly Malloy reined forward, passing his companion and drawing to within a hundred feet of the lead wagon. Then he hailed the driver easily. 'Howdy, partner. How far to Hays City?'

The burly fellow on the wagon seat scowled in suspicious surprise. Shooting a stream of tobacco juice at the ground he scanned Malloy cautiously before remarking, 'Ye're kinda lost, ain't ye?'

Malloy grinned, partly because he realized that he was being spotted as a hard case. After all, a man couldn't live three months with Pancho and come away looking his Sunday best. Still it was funny to have a villainous-looking character like this wagon driver eyeing him with almost fearful suspicion.

'Not just kinda lost,' Malloy told him good-naturedly. 'All the way lost. My partner and I don't talk the same lingo and he's the only one knows where we are. I'm gettin' a mite curious.'

The burly one frowned, not liking the explanation very well. 'Ye're some twelve mile west o' Fort Wallace,' he growled. 'That's a fur piece west of Sheridan—so ye kin see ye're plenty fur from Hays.'

'Thanks,' Malloy said shortly. He watched the clumsy wagons as they churned past him, noting that they were the property of the Prairie Express Company. Apparently Dave Nixon had not yet ruined the company completely with his poker playing.

Pancho and the pack horses went stolidly forward and presently Malloy was watching both movements from the rear. It was then that he noticed the mounted guard who had swung wide from the wagon train. The man was riding directly toward him, evidently intending to speak. Suddenly Malloy realized that he knew the fellow. It was Windy, the poisonous little hombre who had once tried to carry out Brone's murder orders.

Malloy let his right hand drop toward his gun but he kept his glance calm. Windy evidently had recognized him even through the [illegible]

[illegible]

[illegible]

'It ain't likely yuh'll find everything all fun and jollity,' Windy told him, still smirking. 'The gov'ment brand shows mighty plain on the critter and the army has been actin' downright sudden with hombres what run off with their livestock.'

Malloy shrugged. 'He's their horse and they can have him. I had a right to him when I first forked him and this will be my first chance to give him back.'

The hard little eyes were studying him again, something like perplexity mingling with the malevolence. 'Better git a better yarn than that, Malloy. The blue-bellies is fixin' to be right abrupt with yuh when they ketch up with yuh. They claim yuh deserted on the Washita and stole the nag. Ridin' in all innercent like ain't goin' to go good with 'em.'

Again Malloy had to take pains with his features. The statement came as a shock but he managed to keep his voice steady as he said, 'I'll take care of myself, thanks.'

'Don't be so danged sure o' that,' Windy retorted. 'Even with all them whiskers they'll spot yuh. It might be smart to ride into Sheridan and find Carl Brone. He might have some ideas fer yuh.' This time the man sounded more serious.

'Why?'

Windy shrugged. 'Jest a hunch. Mebbe I talk too dam' much. If yuh decided to look him up, though, yuh might tell him I sent yuh.'

He picked up the reins but spoke again as he wheeled his horse. 'The Temple outfit's camped at Sheridan, in case yuh're interested. Mebbe the gal don't hold no grudges against either Malloy or Carey.'

Malloy watched him for several minutes, trying to fathom the man's real intent. Windy's news had been bitter but it had been delivered almost as a bit of friendly advice. Maybe the reference to Brone was the tip-off. Windy figured Malloy as the deserter the army was naming him—and evidently with the added angle of the mixed identity. Brone's gang would be ready to welcome a man who was definitely on the wrong side of the law.

For the moment he almost forgot the reference to the Temples. The old bitterness had come back even while he talked to Windy. Deserter! Was that some more of Walter Loeffler's work? One way or another it was going to make matters mighty awkward. If such a charge had been lodged against him he would certainly be arrested as soon as he showed his face in Hays City.

He turned the situation over in his mind as he rode forward to confer with Pancho. It took [illegible] called Hays, Sheridan and Wallace. Then he pointed to Malloy and cut a quick circle around to Sheridan, indicating that he was advising Malloy to avoid Fort Wallace and strike for the new town at the end of the rail line. Another significant gesture to his neck and the brand on Malloy's mount made it quite clear that he realized his companion's danger.

Malloy nodded his agreement and bent down to shake Pancho's hand in farewell. He would have liked to express his gratitude a little more completely but under the circumstances he thought his friend would understand. Then, without further ado, he left the Mexican and swung away to the north, following the line Pancho had indicated. Regardless of the rights of the matter there was no point in placing himself at the mercy of the unknown commander at Fort Wallace. If he were to have a charge of desertion lodged against him he wanted the arrest to be made in â town where there were civil authorities. In that way he would be certain to get a hearing where he could offer his defense. Since he had not been an enlisted man he could not possibly be guilty of desertion but he knew that a perfect defense would be of no value if he should get into the hands of one of those bull-headed officers of which the frontier army seemed so full.

It was mid-afternoon when he circled south again. In a short time he struck a railroad line and knew that he had overshot his mark. Accordingly he turned west again, fol-lowing the rails until he could see the cluster of shacks which marked the end of construction. That would be Sheridan, a town of temporary importance which would prob-ably cease to exist when the rails were pushed on into the west.

However, it was not the dingy little shanty town which took his attention. Nearer to him than the shacks and tents were the tops of perhaps two score emigrant wagons, fresh white canvas mingled with the stained, weatherbeaten tops of older vehicles. Sheridan had become the jumping-off point for the wagon trains that were assembling for the push westward. Everywhere men and women bustled about, packing, repairing and otherwise getting ready for the season's rush.

Bearded men and haggard women eyed him silently as he entered the spreading encampment, most of them too busy to do more than look. He replied briefly to a couple of gruff greetings but then he caught a glimpse of the trim figure which he had seen so often in his winter's dreams. On one count, at least, [illegible]

[illegible] him. He was within a dozen yards when a man came out from behind a wagon, a gaunt, stoop-shouldered man whose bowlegs seemed to be merely extensions of all The other awkward curves which made up his stooped frame. He opened his mouth to say something to Helen but the words never came. Instead there was a sort of strangled grunt as he looked at the approaching horseman.

'Malloy! What the hell!'

Instantly Helen whirled, eyes wide as she took a second look at the newcomer. Something like a cry of welcome came to her lips but it was smothered instantly and turned into a muttered warning to Andrews.

'Come back here,' Andrews snapped, taking his cue. 'Git outa sight before somebuddy sees yuh.'

The air of worried excitement made Malloy realize that Windy had not exaggerated. He rode through a gap into a sort of enclosure formed by the three wagons which seemed to make up the Temple outfit, dismounting hurriedly as Helen came over to seize his hand.

'Sid! Is it really you?' The words were not a question but an exclamation of happy astonishment. They told Malloy almost as much as the light in her eyes. He had not merely dreamed when he hoped that Helen Temple cared for him.

'I'm me, all right,' he assured her, smiling as he kept her hand firm in his grimy fist. 'Although I'll wager I don't look it.'

He had to release her while he shook hands with Willie Andrews and then all three of them were asking questions at the same time, no one waiting for a reply or offering one.

'One at a time,' Malloy protested with a laugh. The laugh came easily in spite of the trouble which was becoming so apparent. Mcrcly being here beside a girl who had welcomed him so warmly was enough to make a man feel like laughing.

'You tell it,' Helen said quickly, happiness and concern still mingling in her eyes. 'We'd given you up for—dead.' The slight hesitation before the final word brought him a renewed tingle of satisfaction. He had not been unduly optimistic after all in hoping that he still had a chance with Helen Temple.

He told his story in some detail, pausing only for an occasional comment or question as his listeners seemed to be fitting the account into a story with which they were already familiar. Then, without pausing, he climaxed his yarn with a reference to the meeting with Windy. 'What makes people think I deserted?' [illegible] with brisk indignation. 'There was a great deal of criticism when the winter campaign was reported, many of the army officers condemning General Custer for failing to rescue Major Elliot and his men. I talked to Major Gilmer about it and he was greatly disturbed. He wouldn't make an open accusation against a fellow officer but he gave me the impression that he thought Custer was using you as a scapegoat.'

'Why me? I didn't suppose Custer even knew I existed.'

'You're the goat because your so-called desertion broke the contact with Elliot's party. When you disappeared there was no one to report their predicament.'

'Loeffler knew. How do they get around that?'

'They simply don't report it that way. I haven't even heard that Loeffler was involved.'

He smothered the angry words which wanted to come. 'Where can I get in touch with Major Gilmer?' he demanded. 'Gilmer seems to be one officer who is interested in doing an honest job instead of playing politics for the inner circles of the officer fraternity.'

She shook her head worriedly. 'I don't know where he is at present. He has been covering the whole state in an attempt to break up these wagon robberies. The army has lost almost as much as the Prairie Express Company.'

'Like the one last fall?' Malloy asked. 'The one they tried to blame on Indians?'

'Same idea,' she agreed, her frown deepening. 'And I might as well tell you that Major Gilmer puts part of the blame on Dave Nixon.' It was clear that she had hated to make the statement and Malloy wondered just how she felt about Nixon.

'Dave didn't play a very smart game,' he suggested, hoping she would explain without direct questioning.

She did not look up but there was a stern look about her lips as she commented, 'Dave tried to play it too smart.'

'Meaning what?'

She looked up for just an instant, bleakness in her eyes as she told him, 'Major Gilmer says he's tied up with the crooks who have been doing the jobs. Don't ask me for details. I don't even know what they are. I'm simply glad the miserable creature was unmasked in time.'

'Easy,' Andrews cautioned. 'You're tellin' Gilmer's secrets. We don't even know he's shut the trap on Dave yet.'

This time she met Malloy's glance squarely. 'Major Gil-mer told me that by way of friendly warning,' she said. 'Please don't talk about it.'

Malloy grinned through the whiskers. 'All [illegible] waited until I was sure about you.'

He took a step toward her but Willie Andrews brought him up short with a startled word. 'Sid! Look behind yuh.'

Malloy turned to find a cavalry lieutenant studying him from between a gap in the wagons. The man's face was stern but troubled and he was gesturing for someone to approach behind him. It was clear that he had spotted the U. S. brand on Malloy's horse.

'Railroad patrol,' Andrews muttered. Malloy didn't pay much attention. It didn't matter what the business of this lieutenant might be; the important thing was that the man was interested in that horse. Something would have to be done about it in a hurry.

16

The hesitancy in the lieutenant's manner gave Malloy his cue and he stepped forward promptly. 'Good afternoon, Lieutenant. I've got a cavalry mount here which should be taken back to the proper authorities. Is there a remount depot nearby?'

The officer frowned, evidently perplexed by the way his ideas had been twisted around for him. 'There's an officer who can take care of you at Fort Wallace,' he replied after a brief hesitation. 'How did you come by the horse?'

It was the inevitable question and Malloy thought of several ways of evading it. Just as quickly he knew that he had to risk the truth. There had been too much of evasion in this whole mix-up; it was time to play it the bold way.

'I was on the Washita,' he said quietly. 'I was wounded and separated from the command. A trapper took care of me until I recovered. Five days ago I left his cabin and this is the first time I've hit any kind of civilization.'

'On the Washita? You mean you're . . . ?'

'That's right. I'm Malloy—and I've been hearing a lot of crazy reports about myself. I was a casualty, not a deserter. Actually I couldn't have been a deserter because I was a civilian and not a soldier. As to the horse, mine was killed in the battle and I grabbed this one. Now I want to give him back.' He hoped that he made it sound sufficiently matter-of-fact.

The lieutenant shook his head dubiously. [illegible] apparently altered any intentions the officer might have had about making an arrest. He turned to Helen, his warning look concealed from the cavalryman. 'You might look up Major Gilmer, my dear. He'll know what to do if this gets awkward.'

The remark seemed to add to the officer's uncertainty. If he had intended to make an arrest it was clear that he didn't propose to commit himself that far if he could avoid it. He waited silently while Malloy mounted, speaking only when the alleged deserter was riding out to where a file of mounted men waited. Then he said dubiously, 'I'm on duty here at Sheridan. I'll send a man to Wallace with you, if you wish.'

Malloy kept his face straight. He realized that the man was trying to play a safe game, not forcing the issue but still having no intentions of letting anything slip by him. "No hurry,' he replied. 'They got along without the hoss for near five months. I guess they can wait while I get a bite of decent grub. If I don't ride over to Wallace until morning it'll be soon enough.'

The lieutenant didn't argue and Malloy was feeling a little more at ease when they halted in front of a hastily constructed building which appeared to be a combination saloon and hotel. Dismounting, he looped his reins over the rough timber which served as a hitch rack, ignoring the troopers meanwhile. Then he looked up unconcernedly. 'See you later, lieutenant,' he said. Without waiting for a reply he strode into the hotel.

Once inside the door he turned to a front window, looking out to see the officer talking earnestly to one of the troopers. The man saluted, wheeled his mount, and galloped away to the west. Evidently the lieutenant was not going to take too much upon himself. A man was on his way to Fort Wallace to report. Malloy's calm act had kept back an actual arrest but it had not lulled all suspicion.

Suddenly a crisp voice spoke almost in Malloy's ear, the words oddly precise. 'If it gets too thick, my friend, there's a saddled bronc near the back door. My camp's about three miles due north, behind that line of buttes.'

It came as no surprise to Malloy that he turned to stare into the hard eyes of Carlton Brone. Somehow he had known that he would find the man without any particular effort. It was like their strange understanding of each other, something to be expected but not explained. ‘Thanks, Brone,’ he said quietly. ‘Maybe I’ll take you up on it.’

Then he saw that it was Brone who was showing sur-prise. The big man had made the [illegible] a similar offer. There must be quite an organization being recruited.

The’ bulky man’s surprise faded quickly but he had no opportunity to say more. The cavalry lieutenant was already coming through the doorway and Malloy had turned abruptly to aim a question at the black-bearded little man behind the bar.

‘How’s chances of getting a bite of grub between meals?’ he inquired casually. ‘I’m powerful empty.’

The little man shot an inquiring glance at Brone, then nodded agreeably, keeping his glance away from the lieu-tenant. ‘Ham and beans on the stove back there,’ he said. ‘That do?’

His voice almost made Malloy laugh aloud. It was so shrill that it was almost a squeak. Coming out of those ferocious looking whiskers the effect was entirely comic. ‘Fine,’ Malloy agreed, still casual. ‘Trot ’em out’

‘Could you make it two portions?’ the

lieutenant cut in. Then, with a half-embarrassed grin at Malloy, he added, 'I missed noon mess today. Do you mind if I join you?'

'More the merrier—if the grub holds out.' Malloy made it sound easy but he realized that this was the officer's way of keeping the suspect under surveillance. Within an hour or two the trooper would return from Fort Wallace and Malloy had no doubt as to the message he would bring. The next move would have to be made quickly and with due care if an arrest was to be avoided—and Malloy had already decided that he would not take any chance on getting into the hands of the military. Better to gamble on flight until he could see his way clear to a next step.

He caught a significant nod from Brone as he sat down, once more realizing that he understood the big fellow's meaning without words passing between them. Even with the tension of the moment Malloy found himself resentful of the way his mind always seemed to run parallel to that of the gambler. It was not entirely comforting to find one's self on the same intellectual and emotional plane with an out-and-out crook. Particularly when trouble was around.

Brone spoke idly as the two men sat down at a table where the lieutenant could watch the trail from Fort Wallace. He seemed to be speaking to no one in particular but Malloy understood the deeper meaning beneath the words. 'If anybody wants to wash up he'll have to go out to the kitchen and ask Shorty to lend the community soap and towel. It won't be very sanitary but it's all the place affords.'

[illegible] dishes.'

Malloy sat up again. 'Maybe I'd better rinse the worst off,' he commented idly. 'I'll still be bad enough for a nice clean dragoon to have across the table from him.'

The lieutenant flushed, partly because he was undecided as to the humor of the remark and partly because he had been outmaneuvered. He now had no good excuse to follow Malloy from the room and he still was unwilling to come out and declare himself. When Brone covered Malloy's departure with a quick joke the officer seemed to decide that nothing was amiss.

Malloy caught a fragment of the conversation behind him, halting at the kitchen door long enough to assure himself that Brone was talking to keep the lieutenant busy. Then he hurried on through to the back yard, snapping a quick remark at the bearded man as he passed. 'Don't go in there for a few minutes, Shorty. Brone will explain.' He picked up a few hard biscuits as he passed a long kitchen table, adding with a grin, 'Maybe he'll even pay for these sinkers. Give him a good big bill.'

The little man's whiskers parted in what must have been a grin and once more Malloy had a feeling that a quick understanding was passing between them. It was odd that the people who seemed to understand him best were per-sons of dubious character. Helen Temple and a lot of crooks! He'd have to tell her about her classification sometime. Maybe she would think it was funny. Just now he was not so sure.

The horse was in the back yard as Brone had promised and Malloy wasted no time in mounting. He rode straight toward the buttes which seemed to overhang the town from the west, the direction just right to keep him out of the line of vision for anyone in the hotel's front room. Two hundred yards from town he crossed a little rise and found that he could angle off to the west and still be screened. After that he breathed a little easier.

Concealment was even easier as he approached the line of buttes and within a few minutes he was entering rough terrain where the prairie seemed to forget its character. Only then did he let himself relax enough to think about the complications into which his return had plunged him. Life was getting entirely too troublesome, he decided. It was getting so he didn't slide out of one scrape until he was already tangled up in another.

Bitterness at his continued ill-fortune was partly tempered by curiosity and a glow of happiness over the way Helen had greeted [illegible] show himself in civilization.

The curiosity was mostly due to Carl Brone's actions. In some ways the man was an open book but on several important points there was no making him out. Back there in the hotel they had understood each other perfectly with almost no conversation passing between them. It had been the same in Hays City. Still Malloy realized that he knew nothing of the man's real business. He was a gambler, a crook who double-crossed his partners, probably a crook of some importance since he seemed to go out of his way to assist men in trouble with the law. Beyond that Malloy knew nothing about him—yet here he was in a position where he was trusting the man with perhaps his life. It was not a happy thought but for the moment Malloy could think of no other course available.

The rugged country behind the buttes was cut by little draws and streams but a column of smoke helped him to locate the camp he was seeking. Approaching it cautiously he soon found that he was not going to be greeted with any show of welcome. Three men waited by the fire, all of them with weapons in their hands. At first glance he thought they were all strangers to him but as he drew within speaking distance he saw that the short, tubby one was the man who had been Windy's partner in Hays City, the man who had been handled so unceremoniously on the street. It wasn't likely that he would remember Malloy with any pleasure.

No one uttered a sound until he was within twenty feet—looking into the muzzles of three guns. Then he broke the tight silence with an affable query. 'Would this be Carl Brone's camp, gents?'

A squinty-eyed redhead stepped forward a pace as though to establish his authority over the others. 'What if it is?' he snarled.

Malloy ignored the truculence in the redhead's voice. 'Then this is where I light down,' he announced calmly. 'I'm waiting here for Brone.'

'Who says so?'

'Me. Why?'

The redhead came forward another step but the dumpy man interrupted with a doubtful grin, displaying broken teeth which Malloy did not remember. 'Take it easy, Red,' he advised. 'This hombre's got Carl's horse. That oughta mean somethin'.'

'Mebbe he's a hoss thief,' Red growled.

'Don't be a damn fool,' Malloy said, still casual but alert. 'Would I steal Brone's pony and bring it here?'

Red muttered something under his breath [illegible]

[illegible] along for a couple of hours, I reckon. He'll be a mite busy coverin' my disappearance and tryin' to keep anybody from knowin' that he had a fist in it. Some gents in blue uniforms are likely to get plumb curious.'

'Army trouble, hey?' The dumpy man laughed, showing the broken teeth again. 'Seems like he's playin' them blue-bellies fer suckers most o' the time.'

'I hope he don't overdo it,' the third man cut in.

Dumpy gestured airily. 'Help yerself to some grub,' he invited Malloy. 'Stew. Ain't bad.'

'Thanks. I will. It seems like the army has a conspiracy to keep me from eatin .'

'They oughta do somethin' to keep yuh from talkin',' Red growled. 'Yuh gab too much.'

Malloy studied him quietly. 'I just know I'm going to like you, Red,' he drawled. 'You go out of your way to say such nice things.'

The man started up but then seemed to decide on a sneering aloofness. 'What makes yuh think yuh'll be around long enough for it to bother anybody?'

Malloy still retained his calm, the irony showing but faintly. 'You almost make me feel like an outsider, Red,' he chided. 'Why shouldn't I stay?'

Red bristled, avoided Malloy's inquiring look. 'Because I ain't havin' it that way!' he snarled. 'We don't need no extra hands on this show. Every extra split means smaller shares fer the rest of us.'

'Shut up!' the third man snapped, his tone bringing a flat silence around the fire.

It was all so obvious that Malloy made his decision quickly. Something big—and illegal—was afoot; it was time to declare himself in while there was an opportunity to find out things. The information might not deal with his own troubles but it might be something to offer in exchange for the fair trial he wanted. 'We'll let Brone decide,' he corn-merited, not looking up. He applied himself to the stew, pretending to ignore the angry glances being exchanged across the fire. This trio must represent Carlton Brone's big game, the game which had remained such a mystery to Malloy.

It was nearly dusk when two riders came up the draw from the direction of Sheridan. Instantly the little camp bustled into belligerent alertness but the tension eased when it was seen that the larger of the two riders was Carlton Brone. Red swore a bit, repeating his vow that Brone was not going to cut any new players into the game, but the others silenced him as before. Then Malloy [illegible]

[illegible] put on a good act of greeting, talking volubly in an evident effort to let Malloy know the game he was playing. Apparently Brone did not know that there had been a previous talk between Malloy and Andrews.

There was a lot of back-slapping and hand-shaking but in the process Malloy happened to catch a quick signal being passed by Brone to his three hirelings. It seemed to settle even the surly Red and presently Brone interrupted the swift exchange of words between Andrews and Malloy.

'How about fixing us up with your yarn, Malloy?' he suggested. 'It'll save time. Then we can put our heads together and figure out what has to be done to take care of you.' He sounded friendly, almost anxious. If Malloy had not caught the sign passed to the other three men—and noted the way it quieted them—he might almost have been fooled by Brone's manner.

The story of the Washita and its aftermath was told in some detail, the telling giving Malloy a chance to study his listeners and see how they were taking it. Finally he cut it off sharply. 'Now you tell me,' he suggested, 'why *your* friend Windy told me to look you up as a means of getting out of the army's hands.'

Brone frowned. 'You saw Windy?'

'Sure. He's the one who first told me I was posted as a deserter. He said to come to you—so I came.' There was no reason to let Brone know that the actual meeting had been accidental. For that matter Brone was carefully trying to hide the fact that he had offered assistance without knowing that it was Malloy who was the fugitive.

The big man squinted thoughtfully. 'Windy was right,' he said after a moment or two. 'you're in a bad spot. The army wants a goat for that Washita business and some of the bull-boys have picked you to be it. But I'll try to do something for you.' The last came with some of the old heartiness. Brone was beginning to work out his own plans more completely now and Malloy wondered what *they* were. However, he remembered that he was still supposed to be in ignorance of several affairs, matters which he ought to ask about.

'What happened on the Washita that afternoon of the attack?' he asked.

Brone motioned for Andrews to take it. Willie squinted thoughtfully and drawled. "Not much. We. made sudden tracks away from the Injun village as though we had all the redskins in the country on our heels. Nobody seemed to know why. We wasn't licked; we hadn't even been attacked—but we high-tailed it away [illegible] officers of the Seventh. Some of 'em claim Custer played it smart and the rest call him coward. Benteen and Reno had quite a fracas with him about it.'

'That's good. If the army picks me up I'll try to get in touch with one of them.'

'If you get the chance,' Brone cut in dryly. 'You know how it is with Custer. We talked about it before. His enemies hate him but his friends won't stick at anything to help him. They've cooked up a yarn to clear him and they won't take any chances on that yarn being denied. This Loeffler's a Custer man and he's the only one can help you. He won't.'

'That's about the size of it,' Andrews nodded. 'They've built up the yarn "til nobody will believe a danged thing yuh tell 'em. Too many gold braid jaspers waitin' to make yuh out a liar.'

'There's another thing,' Brone added. 'That lieutenant you ducked this afternoon is plumb sore. His man came back from Fort Wallace with a funny yarn. Seems that a Mex had been there and told a story like yours.'

'Pancho!'

'Likely. But he's doing you no good. His story fits with yours but all the army seems to be thinking about is that there's something funny about the way you turned up in Sheridan. They figure you deliberately ducked the trip to Wallace and they claim it proves you're up to no good.'

Andrews nodded soberly. 'Yo' better crawl in yer hole fer a spell and wait for somethin' to break.' His sharp glance at Malloy hinted that something might be afoot which he didn't care to mention before Brone.

'But I'll never clear myself by skuling,' Malloy objected.

'Yo'll never clear yoreself by gittin' into the hands o' Custer's friends, neither,' Willie stated firmly. 'While yo're missin' they kin blame yuh. When yo' turn up they'll either fake up a case against yo' or do somethin' else to keep yuh from spillin' the beans. My guess is that they'll git rid o' yuh'

'I'm afraid he's right,' Brone cut in soberly. 'Any charge will *serve.* The matter of the cavalry horse, for example. Once you're in an army jail you won't have a chance.'

'Mebbe that old Mex "law of escape' dodge,' Andrews added. 'I wouldn't put it past some o' them brass button monkeys.'

'And you've got to remember,' Brone put in,

‘that the Seventh is all split up this season. They’re spread all over the frontier, cleaning up pockets of Indians. If you fall into the hands of the wrong officers you’re a dead duck.’

[illegible] formidable clique of self-seeking officers. Still he shook his head, unwilling to accept the situation as hopeless. Having had those brief moments with Helen he knew that life was standing ready to offer him something fine and he didn’t propose to risk his future by continued flight which might really stamp him as an outlaw. ‘I’ll watch my step,’ he muttered. ‘But somehow I’ll reach civil authorities. It may take weeks of dodging but if I can make it back east alive I’ll get myself a fair shake.’

Brone had an answer for that. ‘Did you forget that the civil officers have you pegged as a gent named Carey? Hays City thinks you killed Vance. A lynching bee would be worse than the army.’

‘But Andrews can vouch for me on the Vance business. He was with me that night.’

‘What makes you think they’ll believe Andrews? You might even draw him into the mess with you—if they even give you a chance to talk.’

'He's right, Sid,' Willie said. 'Yo' got too much to buck. Better jest lay low and see which way the cat jumps.'

17

Carlton Brone pulled an ornate gold watch from his waistcoat pocket, consulting it by the firelight. 'You ought to be getting back to Sheridan, Andrews,' he advised. 'It won't do to have the army boys missing both of us at the same time. They might add it up.'

He smiled genially as Malloy started to ask a question. 'It was a piece of luck that Andrews hit town today just after you lit out. He just come from the east and managed to pass the word that a man had been seen riding east. It put your friend the lieutenant on the wrong scent but they'll soon find out different and it will be just as well if they don't see any connection between Andrews and me.'

'I'm on my way,' Andrews said with a wry grin. 'Stick here, Sid. We'll keep in touch somehow. Jest don't git hasty.'

Malloy walked with him to where the horses had been left and Andrews added a whispered explanation. 'Watch Brone. He's too dam' cute about this. Helen's goin' east on the train come mornin'. She's tryin' to git on the trail of Major Gilmer or mebbe one o' them other fellers like Reno or Benteen. Keep yore nose clean and we'll try to clean this thing up.'

'What's the story on Nixon?' Malloy asked.

'I ain't so sure. She only hinted but it's a dead cinch he's not any part o' the gal's plans [illegible] like to know what Pancho told them at Fort Wallace.'

Andrews had no reply to that one. He simply gripped his friend's hand, swung into the saddle, and rode away. Malloy went slowly back to the fire, his mind not too much engrossed for him to realize that a hurried conference had taken place between Brone and his now silent cohorts. If ever a trio betrayed smug satisfaction this outfit did. Whatever message Brone had brought to them was making them maliciously self-satisfied, especially Red.

'Sorry to have put you to so much trouble, Brone,' he said, studying them carefully. 'If I didn't know you so well I'd be grateful. What do you want?'

The big man chuckled. 'Understand each other, don't we?'

'We do. What's the deal?'

'I'm surprised that you don't know. Or do you? Sit down and we'll talk turkey—now that we don't have to carry on the innocent act for your bowlegged friend.'

He settled himself comfortably and went on in the same casual tone with which a grocer might have ordered a bill of goods. 'On the first count we can drop all the fooforaw about your anxiety to establish yourself as an honest man. You're Carey and I guess we all know it. Regardless of what the army thinks about you you're in bad with the law in a lot of places.'

Malloy did not bother to contradict. 'And what does that do for us?'

'You're a card sharp and a confidence man. Your record includes three killings and a couple of nasty knife jobs—not counting the late departed Vance. You're quite a man and you might be useful to me in my line.'

Malloy accepted the easy indictment without a murmur. 'Are we letting our hair down enough to mention your line?'

Brone chuckled. 'That the one thing I like about you, Carey. You're not afraid to call your shots. All right, we put the cards on the table. I'm running a little bandit syndicate. My boys here do the gun work and I pick out the targets. Sometimes Windy spots the valuable shipments and sometimes I get it out of poker-playing drivers. Mostly, though, I'm getting my tip-offs from Nixon. He found out that it's more profitable to play this game with me than the two-bit poker—when you're not around to take care of him.'

There seemed to be no rancor in the final remark. The big man simply added it as a bit of dry humor. 'Does that explain enough to suit you?' he asked.

Malloy nodded. 'About what I expected. So [illegible] where you stay out of sight. I think we're mighty generous to take you in on a full share with the other boys. Are you on?'

There was so much sardonic humor in the smile now that Malloy began to see the light. Brone was a little too pleased with himself—and the other men were too willing. This was exactly the sort of deal which Red had sworn to oppose. And now he seemed quite affable. On the surface Red seemed to have changed his mind abruptly but Malloy knew better than to believe in surface indications. Something particularly nasty was obviously in prospect.

Suddenly he realized why Brone had brought Willie Andrews into the picture. Using Willie had been done on the spur of the moment, no doubt, a bit of strategy characteristic of the Brone genius. The big man had used Willie to play on Malloy's fears. With Willie to tell the story there would be no question about Malloy's belief in the dangerous situation.

'Count me in,' Malloy said shortly. 'I don't promise a thing. I wouldn't believe any promise you made so I won't ask you to believe mine.'

Brone laughed again, a little too exuberantly. 'It's a deal.'

Malloy let it go at that. He had no intention of turning outlaw and he didn't like the idea of joining Brone with deliberate intent to betray. For the moment, however, there was no choice. The whole show was to be one grand double cross and he would have to take his chances in hopes that he could find some solution to his problem.

That Brone was planning to use him false was no longer a matter of doubt. The big man had been mighty anxious to get rid of him at Hays City but now he was too cordial. The change could be explained only by assuming that the outlaw leader had a use for his victim. It was not a happy realization and Malloy did not delude himself into thinking that mere knowledge of it would permit him to avoid the consequences. He was dealing with men who would stop at nothing—and he did not discount Brone's cleverness. The man had been playing it smart even at the beginning, getting Nixon into an apparently harmless poker game for the purpose of turning the younger man's services to his own account. The fellow was smart—and he was ruthless. Bucking him would be a rough business.

* * *

Sundown found Malloy and his three ill-favored companions many miles west of [illegible] by the other three. On his part he was willing to play it out in silence. He did not even know the names of the men with whom he was riding, having mentally labeled them Red, Dumpy and Hatchet-face. That was enough; barring accidents he would not need to become very well acquainted with any of them.

They camped for the night in country which reminded Malloy of the hills he had traversed that first day after leaving Pancho's cabin. Already they were working into mountain country and the realization was not a happy one. This was the territory into which he had planned to ride this spring—but this was certainly not the way he had planned to come.

The camp was as silent as the day's journey had been. Red divided the camp chores fairly enough, his instructions the only talk of the evening. For some reason the three outlaws were saying nothing whatever about their plans and Malloy was in no position to ask questions. For that matter he did not feel it to be necessary. Every sullen move of his three companions helped to tell the story. They had already marked him for the slaughter.

Next morning camp was not broken until nearly noon and although the ride continued toward the west there was no attempt to cover any such distance as they had made on the previous day. Late in the afternoon they found themselves among rocky hills which were something of a surprise to Malloy. He had cxpected rolling country but instead he was looking at rocky gorges and ragged escarpments which made up in barrenness what they lacked in altitude. Pines sprinkled the more gradual slopes but for the most part the draws were bare and the streams were rushing torrents which tumbled over broken rocks. In a narrow gorge where twilight had made a premature appearance Red called a halt for the night.

'Take charge,' he said briefly to the bony-faced man. 'I'll take a squint at the trail while there's still light enough to spot things. Got to make sure the wagon ain't slipped past us.'

Malloy attended to the horses, wondering what the remark meant. Evidently their program involved the attacking of a wagon but the rest was still a mystery to him. Still he asked no questions. These men proposed to double-cross him in some manner or other; there was no point in hoping that they would give their plans away. Better to keep quiet and act unconcerned.

Red did not return until nightfall, a fact which Malloy found significant. In this rugged country no man could do much wandering around in the darkness unless he knew his [illegible]

[illegible] made no report on his scouting trip. Nor did the others ask questions. However, there was ample evidence of a mounting tension. Red prowled around the edge of the camp for some time before rolling in his blankets. The dumpy man mended gear nervously and cleaned his six-guns twice. The third man spent an hour sorting odds and ends out of his saddle bags, doing nothing which actually seemed to need doing.

At first Malloy suspected that all the nervousness indicated some sort of break expected during the night but after a while he changed his mind. Still he played it safe, not lying down until the others were asleep. Without doubt the morrow would bring a showdown of some sort.

Daylight found the three outlaws more jittery than before. They talked furtively together when Malloy was not within earshot and each of them took the time to check the loads in their weapons. Malloy kept his silence but followed their lead in the matter of preparations.

With breakfast out of the way they mounted once more and continued up the canyon, presently swinging off to the north and doubling back at a spot where the canyon broke into a cross fork. Malloy was wary of a trap here but it quickly became apparent that the others were paying scant attention to him. He tested them by riding for a few minutes with Red at the head of the line, then dropping back until he was almost out of sight of the others. No one objected so he decided that there was nothing for him to fear just yet. The tension was due to something on the program besides an attempt to double-cross Sid Malloy.

They emerged from the gorge into a smaller canyon where a rushing brook gurgled through a cut below the trail. Presently Malloy noted an odd motion on the part of Red. For some reason the squinty man was calling attention to a deep pool which lay directly below the rocky shelf on which they were traveling. A glance down the sheer face of the rock disclosed nothing but a dark pool. There was not even a way of getting down to it from the trail except by ropes.

Still the other men had nodded briefly in response to Red's motion. A half mile farther along they crossed above another curious pool where a waterfall carried the brawling stream down into the lower gorge. Once more Red seemed to be calling attention to something down there.

Then, abruptly, they came out into open country and Malloy could see a pair of riders coming up the slope from the southeast.

[illegible]

[illegible] him even at the distance. It was only as the pair drew closer, however, that he saw that the other man was Windy and that both horses showed signs of hard, fast travel.

'Everything all right?' Red greeted.

Brone nodded shortly. 'Not a hitch anywhere. Been here long?'

'Camped in the big gorge last night,' Red told him. 'I rode over and took a squint at the trail just before dusk. Got there in time to see eight troopers headed west. It looked like our man was with 'em. Must be on their way to pick up the wagon.'

'Good. Light down here for a few minutes and take a stretch while we peg out the deal. Malloy, how much of this do you understand?'

Malloy smiled crookedly. 'I might as well be riding with a gang of deaf and dumb Piutes. These jiggers don't tell me a thing.'

'Good. That's just what I want 'em to do. I'm the one who talks for this crowd.'

Malloy felt that the grins around him were scarcely warranted by the humor of the remark. These outlaws were enjoying something he wasn't supposed to know, something he was not expected to learn. That meant it was time to increase his wariness. He would have to listen with two thoughts in mind. He had to get Brone's instructions and at the same time interpret them for the real meanings which they were contrived to conceal.

'We're after silver,' the big man said abruptly. 'A wagon-load of bullion from the Leadville district is due here today. Soldiers are escorting it in relays. There will be eight men and a lieutenant on duty when they reach Espantosa Creek. That's about a half mile south of here—and it's the spot where we grab the silver.'

'Sounds cocky. Six men against nine troopers and the wagoners?'

'That's where you come in. You and Red make a pass at them as they come to the ford. Shoot over their heads but don't hit anybody. We don't want the army getting tough with us. They'll stand a raid on somebody else's silver but they won't give us any peace if we kill soldiers. I'm gambling that some bluebelly will recognize you as a man they want. They'll chase you and while you're leading them down Espantosa canyon out of sight of the trail the rest of us will close in and take the wagon. Red will show you how to shake 'em off when you've gone far enough.'

Several questions flashed through Malloy's mind as he tried to pick the joker in the deal. He asked only one of them. 'How do you [illegible] but Brone ignored him. To Malloy that was the most important item of information he had yet received. Brone was going to tell a real secret—for just one good reason. He did not plan that Malloy would live to make use of the information.

'We'll run the wagon back through here. It's all rock trail so the hauling will be easy. Back there in the canyon we dump the silver into a hole hidden by a waterfall, then we take the wagon on a half mile or so and shove it into a second hole. That's where we leave it for the troopers to find—empty. They can search that hole for the rest of their lives if they want to. When we're ready we'll come back and haul the stuff away. Satisfied now?'

18

Malloy nodded thoughtfully, trying to get the picture in its entirety. He knew that within the next few hours he would have to face a double crisis. Not only would he have the problem of saving his own life but he would have to do it in such a way as to balk the robbery. Otherwise his legal status would go from bad to worse. It was not a cheerful outlook when the ruthless nature of Carlton Brone was taken into consideration. The man would have no compunction about anything.

'I understand,' Malloy said slowly. 'I'm to be used as bait to draw the guard away from the silver. What happens if the bait gets snatched?'

'It'll be your own fault. You and Red take the best ponies in the outfit and you'll be all right. Better get on your way now. Red will show you where to wait at a spot where you can see the wagon before it dips down to the creek. He'll give the word when you're to move in. After that be mighty careful. We don't want anything to go sour.'

If the final injunction was intended to be a threat there was nothing in the big man's expression to identify it. Apparently he had no fear of having his own double game turned against him.

Malloy nodded again and glanced at the

various ponies. The one he had been riding was a bright sorrel, long-limbed and surefooted. The animal had worked well on the ride out from Sheridan so he decided to make no change even though Brone's words [illegible]

One curious thought went with him. Brone had seemed almost on the point of following up that suggestion about an exchange of horses. Why? The sorrel was certainly as good an animal as any—maybe better. Could it be that the out-laws had wanted to put him on an inferior horse? It seemed likely, particularly when he thought of how a double-cross might be planned. If the horse was to be sacrificed with him they would prefer to lose an inferior horse.

Red was getting restless again by the time they crossed the wheel tracks which marked the stage line to Denver. Malloy could see that the man was fidgeting in the saddle and once he caught the redhead's squinting gaze upon him. The fellow looked away again quickly but Malloy felt conviction coming upon him. Red was the man scheduled to pull the double-cross.

They climbed to a ledge some distance away from the trail and settled down to wait, Malloy more alert than ever. Whatever else might happen he knew that Red was the man to watch. That was the only bright spot in a gloomy situation; he was alert to the main source of danger.

They settled themselves at a spot Red selected and it quickly became apparent that for the moment Malloy had nothing to fear. It was Red who pushed forward to the edge of the lookout, leaving Malloy behind him. The moment of treachery was not yet; Red was in no position to take advantage of his companion.

The delay gave Malloy a chance to consider his own plans. Obviously he had to wreck the outlaw game at the very outset. That would not only break up the robbery but anticipate Red's double-cross plans. Maybe he could pull a gun on the redhead and take him to the soldiers as a prisoner. The only trouble would be that he would have no way of proving his story. Red would deny everything and both of them would be held pending investigation. That was not so good. His own case would be hammered against him and Brone would certainly use every effort to hurt him. They would probably make it all seem like a clumsy plot on the part of Malloy to make himself look good.

An hour slipped by and still no other plan suggested itself. There seemed to be just three chances and the first one was doubly impossible. He would not play Brone's game even if the outlaws would let him. It would mean outlawry and an end to everything. On the other hand he could see nothing but army trouble if he attempted the open double-cross [illegible] that Brone would find some way of blaming him for the whole job. He would be a fugitive from law and outlaw alike.

Which left him no plan at all. He would have to bide his time and be ready for whatever should turn up, hoping that somewhere along the line he would see his chance. He had to escape—and with evidence.

His rueful thoughts were interrupted as Red slid back from the edge of the lookout. 'Here we go,' he growled. 'They're comin'.'

He led the way down to where they had left the broncs, adding a final word. 'Remember now, we ride at 'em, throwin' a lot o' lead in the air. Watch me. When I cut back yuh do the same. We'll high-tail it through here. I'll call the play—and don't git no ideas about foolin' nobody!'

'Whom could I fool?' Malloy retorted. 'I'm nobody's turkey right now, between the devil and the deep blue sea.'

Red grinned sourly. 'Remember that,' he

warned.

They eased their ponies down to the mouth of the ravine and sat quietly where they could see a couple hundred yards of trail west of the ford. 'We'll let 'em git right down to the crick before we bust out,' Red remarked. 'Then we make our pass and duck. Be sure yuh don't hit no mules. Brone needs 'em fer gettin' the wagon away.'

Malloy did not bother to reply. He had made up his mind to take his chances with the army. Maybe it was a forlorn hope but it seemed better than anything else in prospect.

The minutes seemed like hours but presently he could see the little cavalcade approaching Espantosa Creek. Four troopers, one of them a gaunt corporal, rode ahead, followed by a heavy freight wagon drawn by six mules. Two armed men were on the driver's seat while a lieutenant rode close beside the wagon on his cavalry horse. Bringing up the rear were four more soldiers.

'Steady,' Red cautioned, pulling his gun. 'Another minute and we go.'

The wagon took the dip toward the creek and the advance guard splashed into the shallows. Red's voice came sharply. 'At 'em, Malloy! Come on!'

He put spurs to his mount and Malloy followed, content to ride where he could take charge at the proper moment. They were perhaps two hundred yards from the convoy when Red raised his gun and blasted two quick shots into the air. Malloy brought his own weapon up to cover Red but he did not pull the trigger. In another moment those surprised soldiers would snap out of their confusion, [illegible] change his plans abruptly. That lieutenant there by the wagon was Walter Loeffler. Already the stocky officer was yelling orders at his men and spurring his own horse toward the raiders.

Malloy's decision was swift. It had to be. Red was wheeling his pony and the carbine slugs were beginning to whine past them. There was nothing to do but retreat.

Even as he turned to follow Red he knew why Brone had been so confident of his strategy. He had known that Loeffler would be in command of the wagon guard, that Malloy would not be able to surrender himself and spoil the game.

They dashed back into the shallow canyon, Red leading the way and Malloy following close behind him. The disappointment had been bitter but it was no time to relax. Danger was near and all around him now. He could not afford to be overtaken by those pursuing troopers and he could not allow Red any opportunity for whatever treachery had been planned.

Up the winding gulch they pelted, avoiding the fire of the troopers as soon as the first bend was passed. Malloy watched the outlaw in front of him, finding nothing to which he could attach fresh suspicion until they had covered something over a mile. Then he knew that Red was trying to jockey him into taking the lead. For a moment it puzzled him and then he was grimly amused. The redhead wanted to force him into a helpless position yet he did not dare slacken his pace to let Malloy forge ahead. The pursuit was too hot.

Twice Red eased up only to have Malloy match the reduced pace and drag them both back into dangerous proximity to the pursuing troopers. The second attempt brought a few scattered shots and Red had to spur his horse again. Malloy was fully alert now, convinced that he understood the general nature of the plot against him. Red was supposed to leave him out here to be captured. Maybe it was just coincidence that Walter Loeffler commanded that wagon guard—and maybe it wasn't.

Another mile fled beneath the clattering hoofs, Malloy taking a grim pleasure in basing the outlaw's attempts to trade positions with him. Then he saw Red straighten a little in the saddle and he knew that the man was getting desperate. The break was coming.

Red twisted his body quickly, his gun hand coming up, but Malloy was ready for the move. The squinty eyes were narrowed in a scowl of exasperation and hatred and the gun hand moved fast. Mere anger and desperation, [illegible] saddle horn, missed it and fell sprawling to the rocky floor of the canyon.

Even as the man hit the ground Malloy saw what his next move had to be. Now that Red's menacing presence was removed he could take the long gamble. Retreat was never anything but a temporary solution to any problem. He had to get back there and finish this job while it was still hot.

He swung his pony into a branch canyon, climbing almost immediately to the top of the low elevation which flanked the draw on its western side. Behind him six troopers still came at a gallop, one of them Walter Loeffler. Apparently the others had stopped to pick up Red.

He lost ground as he climbed and a couple of bullets warned him that he could not afford to let his pursuers get much closer. When he reached the top of the ridge he regained the lost ground and drew out of range. Still there was danger ahead. He had no knowledge of the terrain and there was always the risk of pocketing himself in a blind canyon. That would be the end. Loeffler was not intending to make a capture.

He found another shallow draw into which he could descend, turning the hunt toward the north once more. The troopers were strung out behind him now, the nearest man too far away for any kind of shooting. Malloy kept it that way until he broke out into the open and found wheel marks which indicated the stage line. Then he swung to the east, following the ruts down the grade toward Espantosa Creek.

The body of a man lay at the ford but Malloy could not see who it was. He slowed only long enough to make sure that those galloping troopers were still behind him, then he spurred up the easy grade which he and Red had descended a couple of hours before. Somewhere out of sight up there would be the captured silver wagon and the rest of the outlaw crew. Brone had worked fast but had not counted on having the troopers led directly to him so promptly.

Malloy smiled thinly. There was grim satisfaction in knowing that he was about to ruin a carefully planned holdup. Under the circumstances even Walter Loeffler would not dare to call off his men. He would have to charge in on the bandits and recover the stolen wagon. Malloy grinned again. What better way for one man to handle two lots of enemies than to set them shooting at each other. He chose to ignore the unpleasant fact that when the shooting started he would be fairly in the middle, a good target for both sides.

He rounded the bend into the little gulch [illegible] Brone turn in the saddle to fire a pair of quick shots. The battle was on.

Then he saw his opportunity. A narrow crevice opened into the rock wall just ahead of him and he swung his bronc into the cut, effectively screening himself from the outlaws and getting out of sight before the leading trooper could turn into the canyon. Now the soldiers could concentrate on the bandits.

He slid quickly from the saddle left his horse standing and began to scale the heights. A pair of cavalrymen dashed by his hiding place without seeing him and he could hear the opening shots of the skirmish. Then Loeffler and another pair of troopers went past, the lieutenant shouting orders for his men to take cover and pick off the outlaws. Malloy smiled grimly and climbed. His hasty plan was working and he was no longer in the middle.

He found no difficulty in reaching the top of

the rock but he had to do some careful crawling along a narrow ledge before he could find a perch where he could see the bullion wagon. Then he saw that the outlaws had taken cover and were firing down the canyon. It was evident that the troopers had already scored. One of the mules was down, anchoring the wagon, and the hatchet-faced man was sprawled in the trail.

Brone and Windy were firing from the cover of the wagon box while a third man could be seen among the rocks at the side of the trail. Malloy thought it was Dumpy but to his surprise that rotund gentleman suddenly appeared on the hillside to fire one shot and dive for new cover farther up the slope. Evidently the man among the loose rocks must be one of the express company men who had been on the wagon. Brone's plans had been thorough; he had bought one company man and ruthlessly murdered the other.

The troopers were out of sight below him but Malloy judged that they had also taken cover. Perhaps it was just as well that the battle had developed along these lines. Of the outlaws only Windy carried a rifle. The army carbines would be more than a match for the six-guns of the highwaymen.

Then he saw that Dumpy was still climbing. Evidently the man was screened from the view of the soldiers below and he was working his way around to take them from the flank.

Malloy held his fire, watching the man closely, and his preoccupation made him careless of his own flank. It was only when he heard the scrape of a carbine butt on rock that he turned to see a soldier crawling along the narrow [illegible]

[illegible] and in no position to use his own weapon.

Malloy turned back, bringing his own gun up even as he moved. He was in time to see the squatty man drawing a fine bead on the helpless trooper. At that distance his own snap shot was largely a matter of luck but the hit was as effective as though it had been carefully aimed. Dumpy twisted to his feet in a grotesque stretching motion, swayed for just a moment and then plunged sideways down the steep incline.

'Thanks, pandnuh,' the trooper drawled, inching his way on across the shelf toward Malloy. 'That gent oveh theah had me kinda foul. Nice shootin'.'

'Lucky,' Malloy said.

'But good. Wheah did you-all come from?'

Malloy chuckled. 'I'm the laddybuck you boys have been chasing. Try your carbine on that big jigger behind the wagon. A nice hunk of him shows from this angle.'

The soldier nodded, a little puzzled but not

letting it bother him. He poked the Spencer over an outcropping and squinted carefully. The bang of the gun in Malloy's ear made his head ring but he grunted his satisfaction at the way Brone jerked and disappeared.

The soldier grinned and pulled his head down as slugs searched the hillside around them. 'Ah'm a right fair shot myself,' he announced modestly. Then his grin faded and he studied Malloy with a puzzled frown. 'How come yo're fightin' on our side?' he asked. 'The lieutenant said yo' was that Malloy fellah, the deserteh.'

Malloy winked solemnly. 'Don't worry about me, Tex. Take another peek down there and see if there isn't a stray arm or leg you can snipe. Don't kill 'em all; I want somebody left to talk when this is over.'

Before the man could find another target, however, there came the sound of many hoofs from the lower end of the canyon. Instantly a triumphant yell went up from the hidden troopers and two outlaws jumped to their feet and ran toward the one horse that was within reach. Carbines spat viciously from the trail below and both bandits went down, the expressman evidently dead and Windy badly wounded.

It was then that Malloy found himself staring into the business end of a Spencer. He had never realized how big a .56 caliber bore was until now. It looked like a cannon.

'Sorry, bud,' the trooper murmured. 'I reckon I gotta take yo' down the hill. Leave yore gun and crawl fer the ledge.'

[illegible]

[illegible] wounded outlaw lay. For the moment he knew only relief that an officer other than Walter Loeffler would be in charge. Then he realized the identity of the major.

'Major Gilmer!' he exclaimed. 'Helen swung it!'

A grunt from behind made him recall the trooper who was following him. He grinned over his shoulder, elation coming upon him. 'Keep your finger away from that trigger, Tex,' he cautioned. 'And be careful you don't fall on me while we are scrambling down the cliff. No use ruining a beautiful friendship just when the cards are starting to come my way.'

The soldier picked up Malloy's gun and chuckled. 'I ain't so sure why yo' got any reason to git so danged happy but I ain't even got her cocked. Don't make me cock her.'

They wormed their way across the narrow ledge and clambered down to the trail, no one paying any attention until they emerged from the crevice. Then Malloy saw that some twenty troopers were gathered in two groups around the wagon and the injured Windy. Without waiting for orders from his captor he hurried toward the larger group, just in time to hear the end of Loeffler's voluble explanation to Major Gilmer.

'But how did the wagon get so far from the trail?' Gilmer asked, open suspicion in his tone. 'Surely four outlaws didn't steal it from your squadron and bring it this far before you could stop them!'

'I'm afraid I fell for a smart trick,' Loeffler explained in a show of embarrassment. 'One of the bandits appeared to be Malloy, the Washita deserter. Not suspecting the other outlaws in hiding I ordered my men to catch him. He led us back into the hills and as soon as we were out of sight his confederates must have seized the wagon.'

To Malloy it seemed like the proper time to declare himself. 'That's correct, Major,' he said sharply. 'Then I circled back and led the men to where I knew they would overtake the bandits and catch them red-handed.'

Loeffler cursed aloud but Major Gilmer waved him back. 'What's this?' he demanded. 'Where did you come from?'

'Up there,' Malloy gestured toward the rimrock. 'I had a small hand in the fight as this soldier can testify. You see, I was in something of a trap. My only hope was to play along with the bandits and try to bust up their game by leading the troopers to 'em.'

The major swung back to face Loeffler. 'How about it, Lieutenant? Is he telling the truth when he says he led you to this spot?'

Loeffier's face was an angry red now. With [illegible]

[illegible] silent troopers. Singling out the man who still held a gun on Malloy he snapped, 'Where did you catch him, soldier?'

'Ah can't say as how ah actually caught him, suh,' the trooper replied. 'Ah went up the rock to find a snipin' post and this fellah was already up theah. He plugged one o' the bandits foh me just when the rascal had me foul.'

'Then he was fighting against the outlaws?'

'Yes, suh. And lucky foh me he was!'

Gilmer shot a glance at Malloy. 'We'll look into this matter later. Now let's see about this bloody business.'

He turned to where a soldier had been working over the inert form of Carlton Brone. 'How badly is he hurt, Gale?'

Brone's voice came before the trooper could reply. In spite of obvious weakness the man was trying to maintain his old flippant pose. 'My last crooked deal, Major. The luck has about run out on me.' Malloy could see the wound as the trooper moved back. A carbine slug had plowed into the big man's side and back, tearing a wicked furrow which had resulted in much loss of blood during the skirmish. Another hole in the chest was likewise bleeding badly and it was evident that the two would prove fatal.

Major Gilmer wasted no sympathy on him. 'Got anything to say about this?'

Brone smiled wryly through his pain. 'I can—take my medicine. I'm just disgusted with myself for dealing with two smarter crooks than I am. Loeffler, you let Carey outsmart you—and then you turned on me. You're a damned coward as well as a crook!'

Loeffler sprang forward, his face contorted in fear and anger. 'Stop that! You can't . . .'

Brone rolled painfully, as though to avoid the fury of the lieutenant's assault, but the movement concealed an entirely different purpose. The men around him were caught unaware as a black derringer appeared in his hand, its ugly muzzle tilted upward for a split second before it belched death at Walter Loeffler. The stocky lieutenant's angry words stopped on the instant. He clutched at his chest with both hands, then crumpled silently across Brone's legs.

Major Gilmer barked a sharp command as men surged forward. 'Look to his wound. See if there's a chance for him.' Then with the same complete coolness, he spoke again to the panting Brone. 'Do you want to tell me why you did that, Brone?' He went closer, squatting beside the outlaw leader as men pulled Loeffler away. It was clear that he [illegible]

[illegible]

Malloy shook his head. 'Your mistake.'

'My mistake,' Brone repeated. 'Bad one.'

Major Gilmer's tone became a little more insistent as he tried to get the dying man's attention. 'Why did you kill Lieutenant Loeffler?'

Brone's smile was ghastly. 'Thought I ought to do—one decent job—before I went. Loeffler was my partner—but he turned on me.'

'Save your voice,' Gilmer said quickly, noting the man's swift-growing weakness. 'Just shake your head if I make any mistakes in this story. Loeffler and Nixon were joined with you in a program of planned banditry. Nixon tipped you off as to the valuable shipments and Loeffler kept you informed as to arrangements for armed guards. Today the guard was too strong for you so you hit on the plan of sending Malloy in as a decoy. That gave Loeffler a chance to leave the wagon with his guards—apparently for a good reason.'

It was Malloy who interrupted. 'Who was supposed to kill me?' he asked tersely. 'Red or Loeffler?'

'Red was going to—kill your horse. I guess—Loeffler wouldn't let you be taken—alive.'

For the next ten minutes Major Gilmer squatted beside the dying man, getting every detail possible while Brone was still able and willing to gasp a syllable. To Malloy it was quite clear that Gilmer had been well posted on this deal; he certainly knew what questions to ask.

Finally the major stood up, staring oddly at Malloy across Brone's now lifeless body. 'You can fill in the rest later, Malloy,' he said quietly. 'After what I've heard here I think we'll be very willing to accept your statements at face value in the future. Stand by now while I see if any of these other wounded outlaws want to whine a bit.'

He strode quickly across to where a quartet of troopers surrounded the helpless but not dangerously wounded Windy. Malloy found himself the center of a group of congratulatory soldiers, the trooper who had brought him down the cliff being particularly effusive.

'No hard feelin's, is theah?' the man asked. 'About me pullin' a gun on yo', I mean?'

Malloy grinned. 'Your job,' he agreed. 'Today I've no hard feelings for anybody.'

It did not seem possible that the long nightmare was over but apparently it was. Walter Loeffler had died discredited. That would put a stop to any desertion charges based on Loeffler's evidence. Malloy thought

...ally given his report on the threat to Major Elliot's detachment.

The troopers went to work at the problem of turning the bullion wagon, using a pair of the captured outlaw horses in place of the dead mules. Finally the outfit was ready and the injured Windy was placed on top of the load. He stopped groaning long enough to curse Malloy, then the little cavalcade started back toward the trail.

It was then that Malloy was summoned to ride with Major Gilmer. The rubicund officer was genial in spite of his bitterness over the Loeffler matter. 'Those wounded men weren't backward about talking,' he announced. 'It's quite clear that Brone worked you into this scheme after plotting the whole thing with Loeffler. Your death would have been the cover-up for Loeffler's loss of the wagon. Otherwise he would have refused to play along with Brone.'

'I figured he didn't want me alive,' Malloy

said. 'There was too much chance that someone would believe me when I told my story.'

Major Gilmer nodded. 'That part will be all right now, I'm sure. The evidence is clear enough—and I made sure to pass the word along to a couple of other officers as soon as Miss Temple came to me with your story.'

'You mean . . .'

Gilmer chuckled. 'She sure did. Found me in camp yesterday and sent me out here on the double. You're a mighty lucky man to have such a pretty girl battling for you. My word, but she was insistent!' Then he added in a somewhat more serious tone, 'It also helped to pick up the information they had at Fort Wallace. A Mexican had told quite a yarn there—and it fitted cxactly with what Miss Temple told me. Even before I got the statements of these dying bandits I knew pretty well what kind of a mess you were in. Quite a tangle.'

'Too tangled to suit me,' Malloy grimaced. 'Brone's schemes would have been bad enough but there was also the confusion over my identity and then the desertion charge. I didn't know just how to go about clearing myself.'

'Your method wasn't bad,' Gilmer said dryly. 'It was certainly effective. As to the Carey matter, I think we'll find that the whole business was another of Brone's clever uses of circumstance. Thatcher Vance was actually on

Brone's trail, trying to get evidence against him for a murder in Kansas City. Brone threw him off by playing up the Carey pipe-dream. It served to chase you out of Hays City and permitted Brone to kill Vance with the fair [illegible] Gilmer grunting agreement from time to time.

'It all fits together, I think,' the major commented. 'And almost exactly as Miss Temple told it to me. I think she had figured most of it out even before I went out of my way to warn her about Nixon. By the way, he's already in jail—if that's any help to you.'

Malloy grinned in reply to the major's sidelong glance. 'I don't think I need that particular help,' he retorted.

Gilmer laughed. 'I don't believe you do. So far as the young lady is concerned you have no cause for worry. She put me on the right trail just in time, practically driving me out here. I'm not sure what she would have done if I hadn't moved in a hurry when she got after me.'

'I'll certainly have to thank her for her efforts,' Malloy said solemnly.

'You'll soon get the chance,' Gilmer told him, chuckling again. 'The Temple wagons were not far behind us when we left Fort Wallace. We should meet them soon after we strike the main trail.'

The prediction proved sound. They had covered less than a mile of the trail eastward when they sighted three wagons coming toward them. Major Gilmer promptly ordered a halt, swinging his own vehicle to one side at a spot where the ground flattened out in a shallow basin. 'I wish you luck,' he told Malloy.

The younger man grinned ruefully. 'I wish I'd found time to get a shave and a haircut.'

Gilmer chuckled but said nothing. A strange wailing sound had come to his ears and he was listening perplexedly. Malloy laughed aloud. 'Warblin' Willie Andrews is worried,' he confided. 'He must be; he's singing the regular words to that ditty.'

Gilmer looked puzzled but did not reply as the wagons approached. Willie Andrews was handling the lead wagon and they could see that Helen was driving the second, her father bringing up the rear. Andrews pulled up short at sight of Malloy, hailing loudly. 'Yo' all right, Sid?'

'Right as rain,' Malloy told him happily. 'Looks like you and Helen did a right nice job in getting help on the way.'

'He didn't need too much help,' Gilmer put in. 'He seemed to have matters mighty well under control.'

He went on to explain in some detail as

Malloy urged his horse back along the trail to the wagon where Helen Temple sat. She met his smile as he drew close, a quick look at Major Gilmer having apparently assured her that everything was going well. 'You seem to [illegible]

[illegible] citizen once more,' he assured her. 'The whole show blew sky high when you got Major Gilmer on the job.'

By that time the elder Temples were hurrying forward to learn the facts and Malloy found himself answering questions that were being fired at him from all quarters. It was not at all the sort of meeting he would have preferred but there seemed to be no help for it. The only consolation was the way Helen was looking at him, her eyes telling him the things she could not say. Just as he had felt that deep understanding between them back in Hays City, so he knew that she understood what he would have liked to say now.

Presently the Temples were satisfied and Helen's father indicated that he was anxious to push forward. Helen grimaced at Malloy, her expression eloquent. 'I guess you'll have to tell us the rest when you get back,' she said quietly. 'We expect to settle about sixty miles west of here. The railroad construction crews are already at work on the place. Maybe you can use it for your headquarters while you're scouting the country for the land you want.' Again it was her eyes which conveyed the important message.

'Sounds like a good idea,' Malloy murmured, trying to match her glance even as he forced himself to imitate the calm quality of her tone. 'Maybe you could even help out a bit with the exploring. I wouldn't want to pick out a location that didn't suit you.'

She blushed a little. 'Then you'd better hurry along,' she warned. 'Or I'll pick the place myself.'

'Malloy!' Major Gilmer's voice came in a stem shout.

Malloy turned, startled. 'What's the matter?'

'For the love of Mike, kiss her! These men can't wait all day—and I think they're entitled to see what they've been waiting for.'

The row of grins behind him belied the sternness of the officer's tone. Malloy saluted briskly and turned to climb up to the wagon seat. Helen was rosy enough now but she met his advance quickly, only murmuring, 'Get rid of those whiskers before you come back. They tickle.'

He kissed her again, drawing a loud cheer from the grinning troopers. Then he jumped down, reaching for his horse. At the same time the Temple wagons jolted into motion and from the lead wagon a rollicking sound took the place of the soldiers' cheers. Willie Andrews was singing—and the tune was unmistakably *Garry Owen.* There was a flat silence as men smiled at each other while [illegible]

[illegible]

[illegible]
a-gun.
Sure it's great when you win but it's hell if
you fail
When you're ridin' along on the double-
cross trail.
Then it's yip-i-yay . . .

Malloy grinned at Major Gilmer as the creak of wheels drowned out the words. 'That answers my last question,' he said. 'Willie did it.'